THE ROARING GIRL

OTHER BOOKS BY
GREG HOLLINGSHEAD

Famous Players (stories)
White Buick (stories)
Spin Dry (novel)

THE ROARING GIRL

GREG HOLLINGSHEAD

Stories

A Patrick Crean Book

SOMERVILLE HOUSE PUBLISHING

TORONTO

Canadian Cataloguing in Publication Data

Hollingshead, Greg, 1947–
The roaring girl

"A Patrick Crean Book"
ISBN 1-895897-53-X

I. Title.
PS8565.0624R6 1995   C813'.54   C95-931536-5
PR9199.3.H65R6 1995

Second Printing

Design: Gordon Robertson
Cover photograph: Barbara Cole
Author photograph: Sheila Whincup

Printed in Canada

A Patrick Crean Book

Published by Somerville House Publishing,
a division of Somerville House Books Limited:
3080 Yonge Street, Suite 5000, Toronto, Ontario M4N 3N1

Somerville House Publishing acknowledges the financial
assistance of the Ontario Publishing Centre, the Ontario
Arts Council, the Ontario Development Corporation,
and the Department of Communications.

For Rosa and David,
truehearts

For helping me to tell individual stories in this collection better than I was doing it at the time, I want to thank Trevor Ferguson, Rosa Spricer, Merna Summers, and Wayne Tefs. For caring about my characters and what happens to them as fiercely as I do, I am grateful to my editor, Patrick Crean.

Much of this book has been written during time funded by the Alberta Foundation for the Arts. To the officers and juries I express my appreciation.

Most stories have appeared previously in a different form. "The Appraisal" was published in *The Canadian Forum*, "How Happy They Were" in *Hearts Wild*, "The Death of Brulé" in *Nimrod*, "The Age of Reason" in *Parallel Voices / Voix Parallèles*, "The People of the Sudan" and "The Roaring Girl" (as "Fina Jim") in *The Fiddlehead*, "Rat With Tangerine" in *The Prairie Journal of Canadian Literature* and *Alberta Bound*, "The Side of the Elements" in *The Fiddlehead* and *Alberta Re/Bound*, "Walking on the Moon" in *The Malahat Review* and *Boundless Alberta*, "The Naked Man" (as "The Story of Alton Finney") in *The Fiddlehead* and *Best Canadian Stories*, and "Rose Cottage" in *The Malahat Review* and *Stag Line*. "The Appraisal," "Rat With Tangerine," and "The Side of the Elements" have been broadcast on CBC Radio.

Jesus said, "Become passers-by."
– *The Gospel of St. Thomas*

There are no innocent bystanders.
What were they doing there in the first place?
– *William S. Burroughs*

CONTENTS

THE SIDE OF
THE ELEMENTS

M Y WIFE and I had to leave the city for a year, were forced to rent our house to strangers. We advertised in the paper, screened people. Hopeless people. If your dog went with them for a walk he would get run over.

Derek worked for a cable TV company, something technical. He could do us a hook-up for free. He had a compact air, like a video component. Frank was more likable. Tall and thin, balding, with fine long blond hair. He worked for a big screw and gear firm, was due for promotion to section superintendent. He had a refined, florid face and red, evasive eyes. He was good humoured, had a soft laugh.

We sat with these two in our living room. They had called first, seen the house first, checked out apartments and other possibilities, and now they were back. The coming back itself was a major point in their favour. Derek was a germ nut, they both said. Always down on his knees, scrubbing away. Frank was crazy about antiques, asked if he'd be allowed to move his favourite piece, a nineteenth-century black cherry armoire, into his bedroom. I said sure.

Frank asked if we would mind a little painting. He had this vintage T-bird he wanted with him but not before he gave the garage a new coat.

He loves that car, Derek commented evenly.

I said I'd pay for the paint.

There was a pause. I tried to explain my position. "The thing about me," I said, "I see the patterns. When you see the patterns you tend to be afraid. So I try to live in good neighbourhoods—like this one. I buy insurance. I go to bed at eleven. I'm married—" I indicated my wife. "My wife and I own our own house. I know what the elements can do to a house in a mere four seasons."

"I know what you mean," Frank said.

"I've watched paint blister and crack and fall to the ground in wafers," I continued. "I've reached through holes in wallboard and fingered foundations the consistency of gravel and damp flour. Once, frost heaved a sidewalk alongside the house and opened a two-inch gap in the parging that ran six feet before it disappeared up under the siding. I woke sweating. I still do. 'If the water in that wall freezes, the whole thing'll blow wide open!' I worry about the roof. Ice dams." I shook my head. "All too well I know the damage an ice dam can do. When I think of that water soaking down through the joists, I could just weep. Or the back deck drifting clean away from the house—*and it is!*"

By then we were getting along pretty well. When I looked at my wife, she was nodding. So were Derek and Frank.

"Sure the house is old," Derek said. "But it's good enough for us." He looked at his watch. "Hey, I guess we'd better get a move on."

I called Frank's reference, his aunt, who admitted concern that Frank should be twenty-seven and still not have found a nice girl. But taking care of a house was right up his alley. I could certainly count on that much.

We gave it to them. They came back the next day, and Derek, who really was a flinty little guy, got the rent down by forty dollars. They handed over the damage deposit. At the end of the month they arrived right on time with their stuff packed neatly in taped boxes.

"Even with you guys, I'm nervous," I confessed. "This is own-ing, you'll say, or age. Experience informs, you get cautious, you get over-cautious, you get paralyzed, you die. You can't be too careful, people say. Don't take chances. But this is advice for old people, who are already being too careful and not taking chances. Trying to pretend it's not all chance out there. On the other side you have the young, who live for chance. Warnings only irritate them. So what do we have? Reckless youth and cautious old age: alien worlds in a continuum of chaos."

"You could be right," Frank said. We shook hands all round and told them to enjoy our house.

On our way to the airport, we made jokes about how those two were so compulsive they just had to be maniacs. As long as it wasn't with the furniture, we said.

In the first few weeks Derek called a few times with com-plaints, little things. A carping petty whiner. He wanted more in-sulation around the front door, he wanted magnetic fasteners on the kitchen cupboards. I told him sure. Do it, do it. We'll reim-burse. I told him I personally—though I assured him not in that house—had known drafts that could freeze milk in a dog's dish. Had witnessed a grown man receive a concussion from straighten-ing up into an open cupboard door. I told him I respected his re-quest the way I respected the capacity of water to seep. No longer was I astonished by how fast fire can spread—

Derek said, "This must be costing you a fortune. Guess what. You have cable now."

Receipts arrived, we reimbursed. For a long time then we didn't hear. The post-dated cheques cleared. Sometimes the house seemed a very long way away, other times I worried. Finally I called, to ask how things were going. Settle my mind. In all I called three times. Twice I got guys I didn't know, who said Frank wasn't home and nobody knew when he would be. Both times there seemed to be a party going on. Horseplay, shouts for beer, the stereo going. I kept thinking their time zone was later than ours, but it was earlier: the middle of the afternoon. Mid-week.

Finally I got Frank. "Frank, listen," I said. "My wife and I are a little worried you're using our home for a party house. You're looking after it, are you?"

"Oh sure," Frank said. "Don't think about it. We've just got a few friends over. The house is great. We really like it."

"Stop fretting," my wife told me one day. "There's not a thing we can do."

At month six a rent cheque bounced. "No problem," Frank explained when I called him about it. "I guess Rod didn't get to the bank after all. Some turkey's got a garnishee on his pay cheque. I'll send another one today. I'll have a talk with him. It won't happen again."

I asked who Rod was. Frank explained that Rod and Sue were the people he was living with. I asked what had happened to Derek. Derek, he told me, had moved out fairly early on. He had brought his girlfriend in, and the three of them had not hit it off. But Rod and Sue and him got along fine. With them things were great.

"Frank, I'm sorry," I said. "I'm a worrier. I'm the kind of guy who keeps up on metal fatigue."

As I talked to Frank I could hear a party going on in the background. This was just before noon on a Monday.

Cheques seven to twelve cleared. I made no more calls to Frank because they were only upsetting me. A year had passed. We flew home, fearing the worst. Beer-fight stains, cigarette burns, milkweeds in the back yard. I tried to call the house from the airport. The line was busy for fifteen minutes. We drove to my mother-in-law's. Still busy. I left my wife with her mother and went straight over. It was the day after Frank should have been out.

There was a party going on. It was Sue, of Rod and Sue, who answered the door. A short young woman with a large bust, she

4

seemed incoherent. I explained who I was. She nodded, vaguely.

"Is Frank in?" I asked.

"Hold on," she said and came into focus. "Bad news. There's been an accident here. Frank's dead."

The party was Frank's wake. She invited me in. I moved through the party, through my house. The air was dense with smoke, laughter, heavy metal. A powerful young man with a crushed nose put his hand on my shoulder.

"I'm telling you, man, Frank was a saint. He'd kiss your ass in Eaton's window. Want to show you—" He pushed away through the crowd.

I found Sue in the kitchen.

"What happened?" I asked. "How did Frank die?"

"You don't know?" she said.

"I just got here."

"Oh yeah." She opened her mouth, closed it. "Hey, Weasel!" she called to someone down the hall. "Get off the phone and come and tell this dweeb how Frank died. I can't hack it."

Weasel did not look like a weasel at all. He was thickset with blunt features. But he told me the story.

On Saturday, after closing the local bar, Frank had come back here with a few friends to watch videos. Sometime before morning he disappeared. No one saw him leave. No one noticed he was gone. He went upstairs, put on his best suit, took a beer from the fridge, and went out to the garage. There he locked the door and got into his old Ford Escort. Sunday and Monday Rod and Sue wondered where he was. Tuesday Rod noticed the garage was locked. Wednesday he wondered why. Thursday he kicked down the door. Frank was badly discoloured by the monoxide. But he had his good suit on and a smile on his face. There was half a bottle of beer on the seat beside him and a burned-down cigarette in his fingers.

"The smile'll be rictus," I said.

Weasel didn't hear. He said it was too bad Frank hadn't had a chance to paint the garage. "Who wants to buy the farm in a Ford Escort?"

"You know," I told Weasel. "Sometimes from behind the paper my wife will say, 'More bad news,' and I say, 'It's always bad.' We're not talking about the nature of news or the nature of newspapers, my wife and I, we're talking about the nature of the world. The news is only getting worse if you're expecting it to get better."

The crushed-nose guy was back with a manila folder. He shoved Weasel aside. "You know what else the dude was? An artist. At work when we sign off? Everybody just scrawls their name? Lemme-outa-here! Not Frank. He'd draw this rising sun, this big smile on, coming up through the clouds. Frank was different. Look at this." He opened the folder to show me, but either he had grabbed the wrong one or Frank kept his best work elsewhere. The folder contained a few centrefolds, several "Readers' Wives" from some less polished publication, and two or three unfinished, amateur sketches of faces, a guitar, a car. Frank's friend closed the folder soberly.

A tall guy with an earring came into the kitchen for a beer. "The thing is," he told me, placing a finger on my wrist, "he tried it before. You noticed the tattoo? The dagger?"

I shook my head.

"Cosmetic purposes. You try once you'll try again. You understand what I'm saying?"

I nodded. Here was a man who truly saw the patterns. If he had owned this house no one would have died in the garage.

"I do understand," I said. "People tell me, Oh how can we live under the threat of nuclear war, and I say, People have always arranged to live under the threat of war. What difference you and your family or the whole world?"

He was in the fridge, getting his beer.

"For God's sake," I said. "Even chimps in the jungle wage war.

Not so much nowadays only because there's not so much jungle. Arming them with handguns would be an act of mercy. It takes an awful long time to die from a chimp clubbing."

"Damn right you would," he said and walked away.

I took a tour of the house. There was new wallpaper upstairs, a Tahitian sunset motif. Green plaque in the toilet bowl. People on the bed, two sleeping, one sitting at an angle to see the TV around the open door of Frank's black cherry armoire. In the back yard the lawn mower sat rusting in long grass like a piece of abandoned farm machinery. Rod, of Rod and Sue, was sitting on the back steps, gazing at it, or perhaps past it. Talking to Rod was like talking to a farmer after a twister. The information that he and Sue were due out yesterday only seemed to deepen his reverie. His reply, when it came, was gentle, almost wistful.

"Since Frank, eh, we were kind of thinking we'd move out anyways," he said.

I sat down on the step beside Rod, and together we shared a moment of silent illumination.

When I stood up I put my hand on his shoulder. "Rod," I said. "Flesh is grass."

He looked at me, startled, but I think he knew what I meant. He watched me go back into the house.

As I was leaving, the crushed-nose guy had something else to show me. It was a picture in a silver frame, a pale colour photograph of Frank behind the wheel of a blue '64 Thunderbird. His elbow and a bottle of beer rested on the door. He was squinting into the sun.

"That was the Frank I knew, eh," the crushed-nose guy said, with some force. "He loved his car and he loved his beer. He was okay."

"He seemed to be a nice guy, all right. It really is too bad. Listen," I said. "I want you to understand. The garage is not going to be a hard place for me to park. Like you people, I feel warmly

7

towards Frank as a man who has chosen the side of the elements. I mean, there's no unfinished business between us. May he rest in peace."

The crushed-nose guy blocked my way with his arm. "The hell there's no unfinished business, asshole. There's the damage deposit that gets paid back to Frank's mum and stepdad, June and Lloyd, right? You understand what I'm saying?"

I said I did.

Next day it was noon before someone answered the phone. This was Sue, groggy. Rod had forgotten to tell her they were moving out. "Maybe we could stay at my cousin's," she said doubtfully.

When we arrived the next morning, Rod and Sue were still at work, tossing armfuls of stuff into the trunk and back seat of a rusted-out '75 Meteor. They left the house in a mess that took three days to clean up, but little was actually destroyed. Somebody appeared to have fixed themselves a sandwich in the kitchen with a Bowie knife while wearing hockey skates, but we had been thinking of redecorating anyway. About noon, as they were making their last trip, Sue told me Frank's funeral was at two.

I took an hour off. My wife went on with the cleaning.

The seats of the chapel were about a tenth filled. People from the wake were there, and others like them, the women attractive in hats and dresses, the men wearing their lustrous suits awkwardly, like uniforms. These are the guys we send in first. There was nothing particular in the minister's remarks. Afterwards we filed past the casket. Frank's long thin hair had been hidden, made to look as if he combed it straight back. I would not have recognized him. He looked handsome, in a severe way. He could have been somebody's forefather.

Out in the sunshine of the parking lot, Sue wept against the chest of someone I had never seen before. Frank's parents were talking to a couple of his friends, so I went over. His mother June was thin and washed-out; when her hand went to her mouth, the

8

whole arm moved slowly, like a limb in deep space. His stepfather Lloyd had an impressive belly, a large shrewd face. A few minutes later I spotted the crushed-nose guy standing alone. I went over to tell him that I had just handed Lloyd a cheque for the full deposit plus interest.

"Thanks, man," he said quietly, squeezing my hand.

I went to my car.

Seven months after the funeral, a cop came to my door. I thought he had come for me. For a while there after Frank died, I was fighting on the side of the rains and the wind and the howling night. Driving the highways so drunk I needed the hit of the tires on the shoulder, the jerk of the steering wheel, to wake me in time. Gaps in next day's recall. That kind of thing. Big pushes for disaster. For Frank. For disappointment, so useful to sustain proper amazement that order should ever prevail. And then one day I watched a child walk a two-by-four across a raging storm gully, and I knew my amazement did not need sustaining.

The cop had not come for me. A rusted-out '75 Meteor filled with personal possessions had been parked up the street for seven months. It was registered in Rod's name. I said Rod used to be our tenant, but I didn't know where he was now.

"To be honest with you, officer," I said, "the guy could be anywhere."

The cop nodded, and in the sadness of his eyes I could see the marvellous structures of our civilization buckling and twisting under the force of sighs and tears and raucous great shouts of human laughter.

He seemed to know what I meant.

THE PEOPLE
OF THE SUDAN

THE FIRST we ever heard about the box, Dave had his arm over the back of the seat ready to reverse down the Gunns' driveway. We'd been standing around on their lawn trying to say goodbye for almost an hour, me shifting Jessica from one arm to the other and Dave staring miserably at Troy and Becky, our other two, who kept going limp and rigid at the same time, the way they do when they're bored nutso. The Gunns don't have kids. Rolf Gunn was going on to Dave about his and Big Elspeth's new Baskin-Robbins franchise, and Big Elspeth was going on to me about her work on behalf of the whales and how it's never too late to get draped.

"I mean, your colours are your colours."

"So what happens when you go grey?"

These words were mine, they had come from my mouth.

"Your colours don't change," Big Elspeth said briskly. "That's the whole point. They *are* you."

At that moment Dave caught my eye, and suddenly I couldn't stand this. "Okay kids," I said. "Time to go."

As if it had been us waiting for them.

By that time the sun was practically down, we'd have to stop at a highway place for dinner, we wouldn't get home until after ten,

the kids would be wired and sleep badly, and Troy had soccer practice at seven a.m.

Anyways, Dave's arm was over the back of the seat, and this was
it—when Troy tapped him on the shoulder. I half-turned to tell
Troy not to annoy his father when he was trying to back out, and
there at Dave's window was Rolf Gunn's face. I pointed at it.
Slowly Dave lifted his arm off the back of the seat. His eyes came
around, and I could see them preparing for what more Rolf had to
say while his left hand rolled down the window.

Like a hound, Rolf tipped his face, indicating the rear of our
station wagon. "I thought you'd have more stuff." From the way
he said this, you would think we had let him down.

"We didn't bring Ralph," Dave reminded him. Ralph's our
dog. Ralph-Rolf, it's too confusing for Ralph at the Gunns'.

"Ralphus," Becky whimpered.

"You'll see Ralph soon enough," I told her sharply.

I could hear the faint brush of fabric like a little gasp.

"Listen," Rolf said. "You people have plenty of room to take
something back with you."

Dave swung his head as if to consult with me, but he wasn't
looking out his eyes. He swung it back. "Sure," he said. "If it fits."

"It'll fit." Already Rolf was walking towards the garage.

Dave watched him for a moment, and then he did look at me.
The look said we weren't in our twenties any more, it said it was
time to stop hoofing and mugging to this particular tune.

I didn't confirm or deny, I just returned Dave eyeball for eyeball, and the feeling for me was the one when you know that everything is about to blow wide open, that you are very close to doing
the one small thing that will break the yolk with these people.

And then Big Elspeth was at my window, which I rolled down.

"Hi again," I said.

"This is really great of you."

"What do we do with it?"

I was watching Rolf come out of the garage pushing a dolly. Tipped on the dolly was a large-appliance sort of box, strapped with steel bands.

"Just call the number for the return address that's written on it," Big Elspeth said. "They'll be literally waiting by the phone. I can't believe how convenient this is."

Dave was getting out to reorganize the back.

"What's in it?" I asked.

"Relief," Big Elspeth said. "From people we know. Wonderful people. People they know are going to the Sudan, and they need to have it right away."

The box was coming closer, and it wasn't getting any smaller.

"Why do you have it?" I asked.

"I remembered you guys were coming down, so I said we'd take care of it. I knew you wouldn't mind."

"What's a phone call?" I said.

Behind me I could hear Dave doing the lifting. Rolf of course has a bad back. It wasn't going well, and then I heard Dave say, "It won't fit."

"There's always the roof," Rolf told him.

It took them another forty minutes to get the box tied to the roof rack secure enough to satisfy Dave. While this was going on, I talked the kids back into the house for another bathroom visit so we wouldn't have to stop right away, but also so I wouldn't have to sit in the car and wait for a bungee cord to whap out somebody's eye.

Big Elspeth followed us inside and stood around filling the bathroom doorway. After a few minutes she said, "Aileen, I just don't know how you do it."

"Do what?" I was wiping Becky.

"Sacrifice your life this way."

I shrugged. "It's my life, there's no sacrifice."

"No, I mean I really admire it."

When we were back in the car, she leaned in the window,

confidential. "Aileen, you're a Winter, I know it. These pastels you wear only bring out the pastiness. Promise me you'll think black."

"I think black all the time, Elspeth."

———————

"I hate carrying things on the roof," Dave said as we pulled away.

I nodded. We were both remembering a couple of years ago driving down the highway, the car slowing down, speeding up, slowing down, and Dave saying the gas line must be blocked, but what it was was the wind resistance as it lifted Troy's crib, which was folded flat and strapped to the roof rack, and then, when the car slowed down, lowered the crib, so the car would speed up and the crib would rise again, and the car would slow down, and the crib would settle, and the car would speed up, until suddenly there was the sound of ripping metal and a wild surge forward, and in the rear-view I saw slats and springs and the mattress and splinters of Troy's crib and bent-double roof-rack strips twisting and elevating higher and higher into the air and many cars in slow motion swerving long before the debris started to rain down.

Troy was with us at the time, gazing out the back window. "That's my crib," he said in a voice of awe.

"The wind resistance will slow us down," Dave now complained about the box.

"Isn't too much wind resistance against the law?" I asked.

This was not a question Dave considered worth even a glance.

As we pulled onto the ring road, he said he never wanted to see the Gunns again as long as he lived.

I told him I could appreciate how he felt, but it was just a box and I'd make the call.

I spent that whole drive thinking about the Gunns. At one point I asked Dave what he thought it was about Rolf and Big Elspeth.

"Pride," he said.

I thought about that for a while, and then I said, "So how could we stand them ten years ago?"

"Immaturity, stupidity, drugs."

"What?" Troy said from the back seat. *Drugs? What?*

The more I thought about Big Elspeth, the more I wondered how I could have been her friend for so long. I thought about my parents and how their friends weren't friends so much as people who amused them, very theatrical or neurotic, witty people, and after a while they'd get bored and take up with new ones. I wondered if I was like that, only slower to let go. Dave, I knew, wasn't like that at all. The way Dave thinks about people, it's a miracle he's not a hermit. For Dave there are the few dozen who will speak out when innocent people are herded into prison camps, and then there are the millions who say nothing.

We didn't get back until after ten.

Dave squeezed the garage door opener the way he likes to do, from halfway down the block, like Batman, and we were tired but otherwise alert, or so we'd have said if nothing had happened. Even after the crunch and the car not able to enter the garage, Dave and I could only look at each other until Troy cried, *"The box!"*

Immediately our neighbours Joan and Ernie were pressed up against the windows telling us how they'd been out for a walk and seen it coming and screamed at the top of their lungs but we didn't hear. It's funny how people will tell you something over and over until they calm down.

Fortunately the roof rack had peeled back as with Troy's crib, so the box was hardly damaged, only our car. Ernie helped Dave carry the box into the house.

"What is it?" I heard Ernie ask.

"Relief," Dave told him.

Meanwhile Ralph the dog was beside himself. You would think

that after fifteen years of unremitting human love, even a dog with an inferiority complex as big as Ralph's would be able to grasp the fact that he has not been abandoned. The kids were wired, it was a restless night, and the little boy I dropped off at soccer practice in the morning was the colour of chalk.

———

The next day Jessica didn't crash until noon. Counting on an hour for myself, I went down to throw in a wash. That's when I found out where Dave and Ernie had put the box. On top of the dryer. Good thinking, men. It was too heavy for me, and anyways where would I move it to? My laundry room is, like, eight by six. I was still standing there staring at the box when Jess woke up, and that was it for my Me time. When Dave got home I complained about his choice of location for the box, but he just went on eating his spaghetti.

The rest of the week was no improvement. The box was on my list, but I ran out of space, so I copied everything onto another piece of paper, everything except *Phone about box*. Not that I believe these things just happen. And then, as I was half expecting, Troy came down with a flu that was going around at school, and twenty-four hours later Becky and Jess were taking their turns on the porcelain phone. For three days it was three sick kids. For two more, one sick mum. Dave never gets sick. And then a long stretch of a week or possibly more and nothing done about the box. I think what happened was, the nuisance of the thing on my dryer eclipsed the nuisance of making the call. It was like when you're carrying four or five things and you pick up something extra. The extra bumps one of the originals, which you immediately lose.

But I did finally act.

First I called the operator, because aside from a Sudan box number, there was just a name and address in this city, an apartment in the north end. The operator gave me the number. I called it. No answer. Over the next four days I called that number fifteen, maybe twenty times. Whenever I got a chance I called it. By this time I was starting to feel guilty, because more than two weeks had passed and I was afraid the people had already left for the Sudan.

And then one day a man answered. "Yeah, what is it."

"Is that Adrian Zignash?"

"It might be."

"Well, this might be Aileen Nakamura." Dave's Japanese Canadian.

I told Adrian Zignash I had a box for him and when would he like to come by and pick it up?

"I would not like to come by and pick it up," Adrian Zignash replied. "The trip's off. Any box is your problem." And Adrian Zignash hung up.

When Dave came in from work I told him about this call, and he said we should drive over to Adrian Zignash's and throw the box through the front window.

"He's on the twelfth floor."

"In that case we push it off the roof."

I laughed and gave Dave a punch in the arm. As for the box, it went on sitting on my dryer. For eight months. By then I could reach around and set the heat mode by feel.

But the box did weigh on me. It may not have been constantly in the forefront of my mind, but at any time of the day I was liable to find myself worrying about it, and when I woke up in the night it was not so much an item on the list—like Becky's asthma, the cuts at Dave's work, my mum's circulation—as a night symptom of all that needed to be done and *let's be very clear about this here in the stark lucidness of three a.m.* was damn well not being done. But daylight smears focus, mine anyway, and what might be absolutely critical at three a.m., twelve hours later is just another nagging worry, and this one seemed to have a lot less to do with the possibility of any kind of practical action than with my totally unresolved thing about Big Elspeth, that other major weight on the clothes dryer of my soul.

And then suddenly it was spring, and one day I was gathering up assorted junk for the people at Mental Retardation, and my eyes fell on the box. Why not? I couldn't budge it, but the M.R. guy hoisted it onto his belly and carried it up the stairs and out the door as if this was something he did twenty times a day. So the box was gone, my laundry room was suddenly almost spacious, and I felt ruthless and efficient but only briefly, because really the box was the kind of problem that retreats to nothing as soon as it's solved.

———

Two weeks later, when I had more or less forgotten about the box, the call came, from a Mrs. Zombo. Mrs. Zombo had the voice of a person who has been living on Camels and antidepressants for twenty years. She called to say that she and her husband were missionaries and that their colleagues in the Sudan had not yet received the box. When exactly had we sent it?

I told her we hadn't sent it. Nobody told us to send it. Nobody gave us any money to send it. I said I had just given it to the M.R.

This information met with a long pause, and I imagined Mrs. Zombo slumped over with a coronary from the shock. When she came back she came back robotic, like voice mail. "You gave, that box, to Muscular Research."

"No. The Mental Retardation Society. Or whatever they're calling themselves now. Institute for the Chronically Challenged. I don't know."

"Mrs. Nakamura, I must say I fail to find such remarks amusing. Your attitude has me wondering if you fully realize what you have done."

"Sure I realize. I gave a box that sat on our dryer for eight months to the mentally handicapped."

Here Mrs. Zombo's voice went flat and dead, like doom. "That box contained twenty, thousand, dollars' worth of desperately required, medical equipment."

I swallowed.

"Do you, appreciate, Mrs. Nakamura, how many people, primarily children, are dead and dying at this moment because of your *unbelievable* thoughtlessness?"

"Nobody told—"

"That box was entrusted to your care."

"I didn't know!"

There was an exhalation of smoke. "You knew that the box had been placed in your care. You knew that Mr. Zignash was unable to take it, as previously arranged. You knew that if there was any problem you could always speak to your friends, the Gunns. Exactly what else did you need to know?"

"I didn't know it was important!"

"But you *assumed* it was unimportant. In effect you chose not to know whether it was or it was not important."

After a while I started apologizing. When that didn't make any difference I started promising. I told Mrs. Zombo I'd do everything I could to get the box back from the M.R.

"The name and address of the purchaser or purchasers will be on the receipt. Anything in the range of twenty thousand dollars will be appropriate."

"Pardon?"

"Twenty thousand dollars. To buy back the equipment from the purchaser or purchasers."

"Are you serious?"

"You do accept responsibility for the loss of these instruments?"

"You think I have twenty thousand dollars?"

Mrs. Zombo didn't say anything then, and in the silence, my heart louder than my words, I asked, "What are these instruments, anyways?"

"My husband will be able to tell you as much about that as you need to know."

"Well, could you put your husband on, please?"

"He's not here. My husband is an extremely busy man."

I told Mrs. Zombo I'd do what I could. I told her it was an innocent mistake.

"The innocents, Mrs. Nakamura, are the ones who are dying as we speak."

"So I'm sorry," I said and hung up and right away started feeling just terrible to have come across snippy about this.

And then I got mad.

By the time Dave arrived home I'd called the M.R. three times, but it was after five and I kept getting their machine. When I told Dave about Mrs. Zombo's call, he clutched his head like Desi Arnaz.

"Call Big Elspeth! Get this Mrs. Zamboni's number! I want to speak to her myself!"

So I called Big Elspeth, who went into one of her *not so deeply hurt as to be spared perplexity* numbers. After a while she came right out and said, "Why on earth didn't you call me sooner?"

"Because we've been hoping that you and your stuffed-shirt dolt husband would pass quietly out of our lives," I might have replied, but not at the time. What I did was I grovelled. I told Big Elspeth, I know, I know, I should have, and I was really sorry now that I hadn't. And then I asked for the Zombos' number.

Big Elspeth said that what I should do was give the Zombos a chance to calm down, and the whole thing would blow over.

I said she was right, it probably would, but Dave did want to talk to Mrs. Zombo.

Big Elspeth didn't say anything.

I asked her again for the Zombos' number.

Big Elspeth said she didn't have the Zombos' number.

When I had understood this I said, "You do know this woman, don't you, Elspeth?"

"Bernice? Yes, of course. But not as a person."

"No? As what then? A tuna?"

Big Elspeth had covered the receiver, and I heard her call, "Rolf, we don't have the Zombos' number, do we." It wasn't a question.

"Whose?" Rolf shouted from somewhere deep inside the house, or possibly the tub.

"The Zombos'!"

"No! Why should we?"

Elspeth came back, and I said, "You accepted the box from people you didn't even have a number for?"

"Well, they were very pushy. If they gave us their number I'm sure we threw it out. After they left we talked about how it had been for us, and we agreed they're pigs. You know how it is with weekend guests. There's no chance to compare notes until you can see their backs."

I told Big Elspeth I'd call her later.

———————

The next day Jess and I paid a visit to the M.R. depot, a bare fluorescent space in an industrial strip mall on a service road. Fields to the south and west. A thin woman in a faded print dress was sorting a big pile of clothes in the middle of the floor. It was a warm day, the front door was propped open, and she didn't hear us come in for traffic noise. When I touched her shoulder she looked up with a complete lack of surprise. You really have to wonder how some people survive. Straight on she was narrow like a wolfhound, with thin colourless hair and a look of ageless exhaustion. I explained my problem, and she told me she didn't know about a box.

I asked her about medical equipment.

She didn't know about medical equipment.

I asked her where the stuff went from here.

She brightened. To the stores.

I asked her how many stores.

She wasn't sure.

She said she used to have a husband, but he drove into a tunnel and it took off his head.

———

As Jess and I were coming down the side of our house to the back door, she said, "Teh-phone!" and then I could hear it too. With Jess balanced on one arm, I thought I'd never find my keys.

"Mrs. Nakamura, *hi*." A voice like butter and cream, silk and fur. A talker's voice, the kind of voice Dave means when he says he doesn't like talk and he doesn't like talkers.

"This is Paul Zombo," the voice said. "How are you today?"

"Okay."

"That's great, that's just great. You people wouldn't be enjoying the same magnificent spring weather up there that we are here?"

"It's a nice day."

"Good, good. Mrs. Nakamura, I guess you'll know why I'm calling."

"I've got a fair idea."

It's funny how sometimes a person will be locked into behaving one way while inside she's going berserk with totally other feelings. I couldn't wait to tell Paul Zombo what I'd been up to on behalf of his box. As soon as I got the chance, I did.

"Excellent," Paul Zombo said when I had finished. "I just knew you'd be doing your best."

"Next I'm checking the stores," I said in a businesslike voice.

"Terrific."

"There's just one thing."

"What's that, Mrs. Nakamura?"

"What exactly was in the box?"

"Relief, basically."

"Well, could you send me a list or something?"

"Absolutely. Well, Mrs. Nakamura, this is a Christian Relief Canada dime, so I won't keep you. But before I hang up I just want you to know how much we here at C.R.C. appreciate your efforts. We're all praying very hard for your success."

"Why, thank you," I said.

I finished feeding Jess and checked the phone book. There were two M.R. shops, north- and southside. We drove out to both.

Nothing. Everybody seemed to have just taken about five aspirins. At the southside branch I made myself so obnoxious I had them begging me to call the director, a nice lady with her mouth full of old money, and she said I should get in touch with the driver. She gave me another number, and from them I got the home number for Wes, with the belly.

That night when Dave came home I told him about my day, and he was not the least bit impressed. He said I should not be running all over town behaving like a person who thought the box was her fault.

I didn't say anything. But as soon as I heard the shower and the yank of the shower curtain I called Wes, who had just got in and remembered right away. "Steel banded? Name Zignash?"

Don't you love the way some people really know their jobs? I asked Wes where the box was now, and he told me it would be divided up and at one or both stores. By now maybe some of it already sold.

So what could I do?

Not much, unless I knew what was in the box.

"I'm waiting to find that out."

Here I looked up to see Dave standing in the middle of the living room in a towel. I said goodbye to Wes, and Dave and I had a big fight that ended in the following agreement: a free hand for me, provided that no money changed hands and Dave would hear about the box only at his own request.

All the next week I didn't know what to do without knowing what had been in the box, so I didn't do anything except check the mail. Then another call came from Paul Zombo.

"Mrs. Nakamura, how goes the search?"

"It hasn't. You never sent me the list."

"Oh dear. Didn't we do that?"

"*Do what?*" I heard a woman's voice with an edge say, right next to the phone.

"I can't do anything more without the list," I said.

"I understand. Mrs. Nakamura, would you mind if we came in?"

Now, it happened at that moment I was looking out the window at a car parked out front, and in the passenger seat a man was talking on a car phone, and I was half thinking that this was who I was talking to.

"I won't pay," I said. "This hasn't been only my fault."

"No, Mrs. Nakamura. It isn't about that. If we could come in, I'll explain."

I told him the baby was asleep and when she woke up I'd have to feed her.

"Of course," Paul Zombo said.

Three minutes later the baby was no longer asleep, because the bell woke Ralph, whose dreams are from hell, and he went into panicky barking.

Paul Zombo was unusually tall and narrow, with wavy orange hair and an enormous tanned baby face like a hubcap. The woman was slim in a slit skirt. She had false nails and a look of permanent dissatisfaction that pulled down one corner of her mouth in the manner of a mild stroke. They seemed to be carrying a lot of things, and I thought of salespeople.

"Mrs. Nakamura, this is Dixie. Dixie's our rock at headquarters."

"I am headquarters," Dixie said, looking not at me but at the case she was setting down on the floor.

"Make yourselves comfortable," I told them, "while I fix something for Twinkletoes here."

I had never called Jess that and had no idea why I did it now. She stiffened both legs and studied her toes.

"No hurry," Paul Zombo said. "It'll take us a couple of minutes to set up."

"Set up?"

"Just a few slides."

"Of what?"

"Mrs. Nakamura, may I call you Aileen?"

He was untelescoping a tube of some kind. A screen. I said he could call me Aileen. "Technology," I said and went to make Jess's lunch. In the kitchen I refused to think what would happen if Dave came home early, whereas a story about this I could shape and time for his less troubled consumption.

I stuck my head around the door. "Coffee?"

Paul Zombo was crouched over a small projector. Dixie was standing at the window with her arms folded, looking out.

"That would be wonderful," Paul Zombo said.

So I made a fresh pot and moved Jess's high chair to the entrance from the kitchen, away from the rug, and brought the coffee and some cookies on a tray, and by that time he was all set up. With my permission he pulled the drapes and used a couple of *Reader's Digests* to prop the projector, which he set on the coffee table, with the screen right up against the mantelpiece. It's not such a big living room, really. I poured the coffee, Jess was happy

25

with her peanut butter sandwich and apple juice, and I sat on the end of the chesterfield handy to her while Paul Zombo hung over the projector and Dixie sat beside him in Dave's recliner with her legs crossed at the knees, looking cheesed off.

"Aileen," Paul Zombo said. "Dixie and I would like to share with you a little bit of what Christian Relief Canada is doing for the people of the Sudan."

The projector light came on and the fan started up. The tray rotated a notch, and we were looking at a green-blue sea dotted with sailboats. A blue sky.

"Now, this is the Red Sea, from the beach at Port Sudan."

"It's so *blue*," I said.

There was a sort of embarrassed pause, and Paul Zombo said, "It's never actually been red, you know."

At this point I noticed Dixie scowling at him, and I liked her then.

The tray rotated. We were looking down a beach. It was amazingly lush, so lush that Dixie seemed to jolt slightly in her chair.

"I never imagined the Sudan would be so lush," I said.

"It's the wrong tray," Dixie said.

"I don't think so, Dixie," Paul Zombo replied kindly. "Port Sudan was remarkably green. This is still the coast, remember."

The tray rotated. Another view of the sea. Very blue.

"Wrong tray," Dixie said and stood up.

"The Red Sea," Paul Zombo replied quickly but firmly. "The coastline really is quite low, but the Red Sea isn't shallow at all. Scholars now believe the Israelites crossed farther up, Aileen, at the Gulf of Suez. See those boats? Crafts very much like the ones you see here have been in continuous use since the days of the Pharoahs."

"Wake up and smell the coffee, Paul," Dixie said. "Those are windsurfers."

"Of course today, with the Suez Canal," Paul Zombo continued, raising his voice a little, "the Red Sea has become a major shipping route. It's a wonder there isn't an international tanker perched somewhere on the horizon."

The tray rotated. A white hotel, taken from the street. *El Cid.*

The tray rotated. A sun setting into the sea.

The tray rotated, and a block-faced woman in a lavender mumu, a cigarette in one hand, stood looking uncomfortable against a whitewashed wall.

"How'd this get in here?" Paul Zombo wanted to know.

Dixie plunked back down in Dave's chair. In a singsong she said, "Looks like the Yucatan tray to me."

"Must be strays. That's my wife Bernice, Aileen. This is one from our holiday last winter, in Mexico."

The tray rotated, and we saw American tourists walking on a beach.

"Paul, this is dumb. The lady is not interested in your holiday in Mexico."

Paul Zombo turned to me. "Aileen, looks like somehow we've grabbed the wrong slides here. But what say, now that we're all set up, we just go ahead?"

I glanced around at Jess, and she seemed game. "Fine with us," I said.

"Okay, Dixie?" Paul Zombo said. "Why don't we just?"

"Just what, Paul? Just exactly what? Just sit here and look at your fucking holiday slides?" Dixie turned suddenly to me. "Look, can I smoke?"

"Actually, Dixie, there's the baby." I knew with Dave's nose he'd pick up cigarette right away. "Would the front step be okay?"

"Forget it."

The tray rotated to a market scene. "Now this one," Paul Zombo said, "could have been taken anywhere." He crossed to the screen. "That is, racial type and costume aside. And produce. The wares, on the other hand, are fairly similar. And a Sudanese market would be just as crowded, easily, as what you see here. Of course, the vendors have less to sell, what with the drought and the famine and the social chaos—the country's been in a state of civil war for almost thirty years, you realize—but the people do come. Of course, they don't have a lot of choice. The whole operation is a drabber, dustier, dingier matter altogether."

Paul Zombo returned to the projector. The tray rotated.

"Ah yes. Now, this is the view from our hotel room. See how that point of land sort of embraces the bay? It really is a natural harbour. You don't get the big breakers there that you get farther along in either direction. Still, hey—" He was back at the screen, pointing. "What's this?"

"Surfers," I said.

"Now, surfers you definitely won't see a lot of in the Sudan."

"Well *duh*," Dixie said.

Paul Zombo was looking at me. "The most heart-breaking thing about the Sudan, Aileen, I mean aside from the West doing nothing, is the kids in the south. For years now, thousands of homeless Dinka children have been wandering the countryside from camp to camp. When the government bombs come they move on. These are children, Aileen. Living worse than cattle, like *hunted* cattle—" Here Paul Zombo's voice broke. He took a handkerchief from his pocket and wiped his eyes.

Dixie had twisted around in her chair. "It's not right what's happening in that godforsaken shit hole," she told me.

The tray rotated. A hotel room.

Paul Zombo cleared his throat. "Nothing at all like our quarters in Khartoum, believe me. Khartoum is the capital of Sudan, Aileen. It and the north are ruled by Muslim fundamentalists. Quite the extremists, in fact. Ethnic cleansers, if you're familiar with that term. Anyway, it was forty in the shade, a merciless sun. But the worst part, worse than the heat and the dust, was the nervous kids with AK-47s, and I do mean kids, thirteen-, fourteen-year-olds, it was incredible, waking us in the night."

The tray rotated to a picture of two couples, one of them definitely Paul and Bernice Zombo, with their arms around each other's shoulders. The woman on the end was doing a spiritless chorus-line kick. The Zombos looked abject and sozzled.

"This is just some people we met," Paul Zombo said.

The tray rotated to an alarming one of Mrs. Zombo foreshortened, taken from the foot of the bed. She was on her back, buck naked, with her legs slightly parted and her eyes closed. In her left hand was a hair dryer, directed at the shifted mass of her left breast.

"I don't believe this," Dixie said.

"How'd that one get in here?" Paul Zombo wondered. He seemed to reflect a moment. "Bernice uses a hair dryer on her body to get herself to sleep, Aileen. When she was little her parents fought all the time. The blower also shut out the sound of that. I thought it would make a cute picture."

"Awful cute," Dixie said.

Jessica wanted out of her chair. I went to unclip her.

The tray rotated then rotated again fast before I could look around. When I did I saw a young Mexican in the bow of a boat, grinning wildly.

"For God's sake, Paul. Haven't we seen enough?"

"This is good old Amerigo," Paul Zombo said. "He took a gang of us out in his boat one day to do a bit of snorkeling. Ever since I was a kid, Aileen, I've had this thing about how many fingers people have. Paintings, real life—well, to make a long story short, Amerigo had six! Number six was growing out the side of his baby finger, like a little sausage—"

Paul Zombo was pointing at the edge of his hand and looking at me as if I should say something—but what?

"You know, here, Aileen, the doctors would whip that finger off within hours. Not there." He shook his head, remembering.

The tray rotated, and we were back to the first slide. Paul Zombo switched off the projector. "That's it, everyone."

29

"Already?" Dixie went out to the front step for a smoke.

As Paul Zombo was packing up, I asked him what had been in the box.

"Relief!" Dixie called through the screen door.

Paul Zombo held up his hands. "Aileen, you've done enough. I'd say the box is now back in our court."

He stepped closer, confidential. "Listen, I'm sorry about Dixie. She's got a good heart, but she can be a little rough sometimes. Poor kid hasn't had an easy life."

"That's enough, Paul!" Dixie called. "You can stop talking about me any time!" She had one of those voices that go harsh when they're raised.

A few minutes later they were back in the car, and Paul Zombo called to thank me again for the twenty dollars I'd given towards Christian Relief Canada's work in the Sudan. I told him he was welcome. He waved goodbye, but I don't think he could see me for the reflection off our window, because he turned immediately to say something to Dixie as she pulled away.

———————

Three days later a short guy with a Beatle haircut and an unfinished child's face cherry red with eczema rang the bell.

"Hello, I'm looking for an Aileen Nakamura. She a tenant of yours?"

I get this all the time. When I told him she was me, his brow darkened as if this was impossible. "I'm Craig Storch," he said. "I represent an organization called Christian Relief Canada. My clients have instructed me to give you this." He produced an envelope.

I told Craig Storch to slide his envelope under the screen door.

What it was was a notice, signed by Bernice Zombo and copied to me with the compliments of Paul Zombo, informing Rolf and

Elspeth Gunn of 4167 Spruceway Blvd., etc., that Christian Relief Canada was suing them for $5,145.00, the estimated value of the goods that had been entrusted to their care.

The next day I got a call from Big Elspeth, a vile torrent that surged down the line like a sewer back-up. Normally I'd have gone to jelly on springs and worked away to smooth everything over. This time I just listened. In Grade Seven I had a teacher who said you don't know a thing until you can say it, but he must have been thinking of something else. I couldn't explain Big Elspeth, not then, not now, couldn't begin to, but since that one time I listened to her I don't have any more confusion. I'm sure there'll be reasons for how she is, good reasons, but fuck her, you know what I mean? And I don't have any negative feelings at all when I say that.

So anyways, on Saturday night Dave and I stayed home, and after I got the kids down, he made popcorn and opened a couple of beers, and when I thought he was ready for it I told him the story of Paul Zombo and Dixie and Craig Storch and the call from Big Elspeth, and he asked the kinds of questions he asks when he's interested, good questions, and we had a high old time. Since Big Elspeth's call the Gunns aren't speaking to us, and the other good thing that's come of the box is, it's got our asses in gear about adopting a child overseas, the way you can, for so much a month. It may not be a lot in the scheme of things, but as Dave says you do what you can do.

ROSE COTTAGE

I N THE AUTUMN Alex moved to Vancouver and got a job driving a cab, because a woman he had fallen in love with was taking classes at Simon Fraser, but in the spring she grew tired of him and asked him to move out. One day, weeping over some little thing, he answered in his neat hand an ad in the *Province* and ten days later was offered, for a small rent, a home on Vancouver Island.

Rose Cottage was a single-storey frame building with a concrete floor and white plaster walls and ceilings. Seventy years earlier it had been built against the east wall of Rose House for the use of the groundskeeper and his daughter, a servant in the main residence. Rose House was a stone mansion with a view of the ocean. It was now owned by a trust company in the name of a beautiful raw-faced widow of seventy-two named Lady Beatrice Cooper, who at some time before a succession of small strokes had damaged her brain specified that Rose Cottage should always be rented to a Canadian writer. Alex became the latest in a shabby line. He was not a writer but said he was when he answered the ad because he had always enjoyed the confidence that he could be. Who was to gainsay him?

Supported on the arm of Nurse Cheam—an ex-British Army matron fitted with a globular auburn hairpiece—Lady Cooper would yearn towards Alex and say, "Now . . . sun . . . go! . . . solla solla . . . so . . . heh heh heh!"

And smiling and gentlemanly Alex would take her hand and address her with a smiling courtly complaisance and a sort of mock obsequiousness, which though kind enough was overbearing and left him feeling like a bully. Other people's realities had always been too much for Alex, and it seemed to him logical in an unfair way that when the damaged eyes of Lady Cooper came to rest upon his face he should respond with a reality that was too much. In fact Lady Cooper's eyes were not damaged. It was the wrongness of such desolation in such proximity to that simpering mouth, the way her eyes seemed, so immediately, from a place so wrecked, to beseech him. With Lady Cooper, Alex was as much at a loss as with anyone how to behave in a way he could live with afterwards, but in her case it galled him more because with her his behaviour felt callous and wrong and not merely, as usual, half invisible.

And then one Sunday in July, six weeks after Alex had moved to Rose Cottage, he planned a day's walk through the forest that stretched from the back gate of Rose House for miles and miles along the sea. In anticipation of this adventure he ate magic mushrooms, an entire handful of the shrivelled leathery bitter gorge-heaving tiny fungi from a Ziploc bag that a sixty-year-old hippy with a yellowing ponytail had given him the previous Christmas Eve instead of cab fare. The idea was a day-long forest walk by the sea, on mushrooms. The idea was, like Wordsworth, to travel out and at the same time to travel in. Alex was not a writer, but he did sometimes feel liable to his own lies. But he was even more a novice at mushrooms than he was at Wordsworth, he didn't understand that the poisons released in his brain would take the straightforward thing he planned to do and deck it with obstacles.

The first was getting out the door of Rose Cottage. What happened was, Alex's preparations for that sea walk crumbled and the pieces multiplied. One stack of pieces toppled the next as beyond the rapidly unthinkable threshold that walk by the sea loomed ever larger and more daunting, with Alex now in one room of the little cottage and now in another.

After that came a long stretch of getting out the door but missing actually doing it. Alex would look down at the flagstone walk then back around behind him and remember the click of the door. Nothing more. An inauspicious beginning, it would seem to him, to have passed unwitnessed like that. And so he would go back inside and try again. Maybe that time he would notice he had forgotten to, say, wear a hat. A hat? What did he want with a hat? Well, what if it rained? Another complicated issue, with much searching, many stages, no hat to be found, did he own a hat? Had he ever owned a hat? And with nothing resolved or accomplished, the minute hand sweeping, he would turn to something completely different and in the middle of that, fall into abstraction *sea walk looming* from which he would rouse himself as from a century of sleep in order to set about a new inconclusive task and suddenly be outside looking down at the flagstone walk beneath his feet and back at the door, the click having sounded behind him— until he thought, "I'll be here all day," and with a brutal focus of will *sea walk looming* shouldered aside all misgivings and moved out through the gate in the hedge of caragana onto the crushed white gravel of the courtyard, by now in a state similar to the adrenalization of one who knows that in the next instant he will be in a terrible car accident, crossing the bounding white gravel *sea walk looming* against an anxious seething canvas of slow-motion detail, out of which, with the astonishment that only utter predictability, as in a dream, can provide, there emerged the eyes, grey-blue, of Lady Beatrice Cooper, bobbing alongside the spherical peruke of Nurse Cheam, and from the back of Alex's head he could feel the spectra go peeling as too swiftly, apparently, *sea walk looming* he bowed to kiss Lady Cooper's ancient princess cheek and to tuck her other arm into his. Sea walk looming.

"Well, well . . . san . . . mol . . . *tuh*! . . . heh heh . . . what . . . ah! . . . now now now . . . tel!"

"Good morning, Alex!" Nurse Cheam shouted. "You look like the cat that swallowed the canary this morning!"

Alex had never thought of himself as a cat before. He did now.

"Isn't it lovely!" Nurse Cheam cried.

It?

"You haven't come to take away my little girl, have you?"

He missed the next part.

And then Nurse Cheam was telling him, as she often did, about the young men interested in herself when she was "a slip of a girl."

But Alex must have missed the next part as well, because all of a sudden he heard, ". . . and when you come back I'll give you a lovely soft, fresh scone and a big tumbler of ice-cold whole milk!"

"Goodbye, Nurse Cheam. Goodbye, Lady—"

"No, no! Take her arm! You must take her arm! Promise me you won't go far!"

". . . yes—"

Nurse Cheam was returning to the house.

"Where would you like to go, Lady Cooper?" Alex's voice asked as the hairs that grew from his skull passing again and again through his fingers seemed to be cilia that had bolted and died.

"Wa . . . wa . . . heh heh!"

"Yes," Alex said. "We'll do that." He drew himself up.

Immediately then, Alex and Lady Cooper were among roses, gazing together as if at a piece of statuary at Leadbeater, the gardener, a lean, toothless, small man with eyebrows like hanging gardens neglected and droughty. Leadbeater stood hoe in hand gazing off at forty-five degrees, as he always did when being addressed, and Alex caught a fading trace of his own voice having said, "Nice day, Leadbeater."

36

"Yup," Leadbeater now replied, darkly, and scowled at the heavens. "And we'll pay fer it."

Leadbeater's retributionist view of the weather seemed to tickle Lady Cooper. "Pay!" she cried. "Pay! Pay! Heh *heh*!"

Next, she and Alex were standing at the foot of the red pine by the gate to the forest. A whispering from above. Alex looked up to see each needle on that tree stir green against the sky. The clouds were three-dimensional and white and moving very fast. Dizzy, Alex lowered his eyes to Lady Cooper's, which were pleading.

"What," Lady Cooper said. "What . . . what . . ."

"What, what," Alex replied. Again he looked up. One thing, anyway, was trees: their size, the stubborn alien familiarity of their unutterable strangeness.

"Who," said Lady Cooper.

Alex looked at her. It was a beautiful old face that had been infantilized by cataclysms of blood.

"Who?"

"Who, *heh*!"

"Who! Who made this tree? Did you make this tree, Lady Cooper?"

"Oh no no!" she cried with alarm. "*No, no, no!*"

But Alex had stepped away from her to reach his arms around the trunk. "Isn't it beautiful?" he said. "Isn't it . . . *great?*"

"What," said Lady Cooper. "What . . . what will . . ."

"What will," Alex said, and he gazed at her over his shoulder as he squeezed the tree with his cheek pressed foolishly against the curling, pinkish bark.

"What," said Lady Cooper. "What will . . . what what . . ."

"Tree, Lady Cooper!" Alex cried. "*Tree!*"

He gazed at her, but her eyes in their monkey sadness were averted down the garden towards Rose House as her fingers knotted and unknotted the air at her waist.

"What will," she said.

Alex let go of the tree. In the same instant that sea walk was right there, all around them, looming, shadowing everything, and Alex understood the depth and extent of his error, that he should ever have allowed this walk with Lady Cooper to eclipse, to pre-empt, that sea walk, which was now back. Not amused. Not in the least amused. How could he have forgotten?

"What will," Lady Cooper said.

"What will," Alex sighed.

One stream of Alex's thinking was saying that he really should return her to Rose House and get on with what this was supposed to be about. Another stream of his thinking was busy with a more abstract debate, one side arguing that a person needs to stick to what he intends because what else can he do? The other side arguing that if there is a single common denominator of human stupidity it is inflexibility. At some point during this debate Alex glanced at his watch without taking in the time, not that he would have known what time it was supposed to be. As he did so he caught sight of a third stream of thinking, to the effect that there is not only what you have to do, there is when you have to do it.

"What will," Lady Cooper said.

Alex turned to her. "Lady Cooper," he said. "I have to take you back now. I—"

"*No no! No no!*"

"Oh yes—"

But even as he was turning her to face the house, Alex understood that he had already missed the necessary time of setting out on his sea walk. It was now behind them, it had passed.

"Damn," Alex said quietly, and louder, "Damn," and he watched himself from above as like some generic mammal he shot frustrated little downward glances to the left and to the right.

"Damn!" said Lady Cooper. "*Heh.*"

Alex continued to live at Rose Cottage through the fall. As the days became darker and autumn turned to winter, he spent more and more time walking, on the forest paths among the great estates and under the old trees where the park authorities had placed benches for views of the sea and where the undergrowth was crisscrossed with hundreds of footpaths and bridlepaths. Many girls and women rode there, and when a footpath intersected a bridlepath, or when Alex strayed onto a bridlepath, the girls and young women would gallop past, pretending not to see him, while the older women would sing "Glorious morning!" from their high English saddles, and he would fall in love with them all.

Sometimes Alex would be crossing the courtyard of Rose House, headed for the ancient trees and the paths along the sea, and all would be quiet in the great stone residence. But as often a window—usually on the second floor—would swing open on the back of Nurse Cheam's arm, and she would lean out and call Alex inside for a nice tumbler of "icy-fresh whole milk!"

Sometimes Alex, not wanting to refuse every time, would accept Nurse Cheam's invitation, and then he would stand on the front step until she opened the door and told him to go through into the sitting room, and there in the chill of the morning he would find Lady Cooper strapped into her big metal chair with the tray, dozing, and he would stand by the window and look down the lawn and the cypress walk at the weather until Nurse Cheam came in with a tray of milk and biscuits to talk to him in her loud lonely voice, the first sound of which would startle Lady Cooper into a soft babble against the din of it.

Sometimes from an upper window of Rose House as he was crossing the courtyard Alex would hear Nurse Cheam shout at Lady Cooper. Usually the sound was muffled, but sometimes he would hear *"Bad girl!"* or *"Don't you dare!"* Once he heard what sounded like slaps. Sometimes when Nurse Cheam had him in for milk and biscuits, she would refer cheerily to their "little boxing matches."

And then one morning, as Alex was eating breakfast, Nurse Cheam came to the door of Rose Cottage to ask for his help. She sometimes did this when she needed a chore done that she could not do herself or that she considered man's work, such as climbing a stepladder or tightening a hinge. Normally she used Leadbeater for these purposes, but when Leadbeater was not around or when Alex's height was an advantage she came to him. It wasn't often—no more than once every couple of weeks—and Alex hardly minded. He could see that she was very lonely.

On this morning, Alex didn't even think to ask what it was, though there was something odd about Nurse Cheam's manner, a kind of suppressed excitement. But he followed her obediently out into a cold drizzle, through the gate in the caragana hedge, along the perimeter of the courtyard into the darkness of Rose House, and up the oak staircase from the main hall. It was Alex's first visit to the second floor. By the time they reached the landing he could hear Nurse Cheam breathing hard. But along the hallway her pace did not diminish, and when she reached the far door, she pushed it open and stood back and waited significantly. Thinking now that Lady Cooper must have fallen, Alex entered a dim room where the smell of urine was thick and stale, and where, at the head of an enormous bed, he saw her white hair, whiter than her sheets, her rosy face, so small against the enormous pillow, watching him as he came towards her. She was making sounds, but it wasn't her soft gabble, it was a kind of whimpering, and he could see that her eyes were terrified.

"Good morning, Lady Cooper," Alex said as he came alongside the bed. "Are you all right?"

"There's nothing wrong with her," said Nurse Cheam, and coming up the other side of the bed she reached for a corner of the bedclothes and in one movement pulled them entirely clear of the old woman. "She refuses to get out of bed," Nurse Cheam said, as Lady Cooper writhed in an anguish of humiliation and confusion.

"You'd think she was waiting for a handsome young man to put his thing in her."

In the time it took Nurse Cheam to say this, Alex's eyes consumed Lady Cooper's nakedness, from her pubic tuft to her lolling breasts to her wrists and neck, where an old woman's creased brown and exposed flesh paled suddenly to a smoothness that time and light had hardly damaged. It was not a young woman's body with an old woman's hands and face, it was an old woman's beautiful body plumped for slaughter, too ripe, too right for exactly this and still more terrible violation.

"Cover her up," Alex muttered as one hand reached back blindly for the bedclothes at the foot of the bed, and when he looked to Nurse Cheam he saw the expression on her face and knew that she knew, and he could see the grim, righteous pleasure she took in the shame that she had so easily brought upon them both.

———

One warm, sunny morning not many days later, Alex knocked at the front door of Rose House. When Nurse Cheam saw who it was she cried in something like relief, "Good morning, Alex! Won't you come in and have tea with us?"

So Alex took tea with Nurse Cheam and Lady Cooper, who was slumped in her chair with the tray, near a low fire in the high-ceilinged, chilly sitting room of Rose House, with a grey light coming through the lead-paned window that faced west down the cypress walk. And after tea Alex took Lady Cooper outside for her morning turn in the garden, except that at the gate to the woods he said, "Where would you like to go, Lady Cooper?"

"Walla. Walla. *Heh!*"

"The woods? Shall we walk in the woods?"

Always when Alex walked with Lady Cooper in the grounds of Rose House there would come a point when she wanted to keep on, to circle the rose bushes one more time, and he would have to say no, they really must go back to the house. But this time he had called on her because he had decided to let her lead him where she wanted, for as long as she wanted. Before her strokes she must have known this forest better than he did now. Alex's idea was that she would communicate with him by the paths she would choose.

And so the two of them set out, and at every junction of the paths, Lady Cooper knew exactly which one she wanted. They crossed a road and another road and still they continued on. But they were moving away from the sea into recent suburban developments, and Alex understood that the old woman was walking in a straight line away from Rose House towards the city, that she did not intend to diverge, that these were not her favourite paths, had nothing to do with memory or the woman she once was, this was now, this was escape.

Not long after he realized this, Alex knew they had to turn back. He could tell from the weight on his arm that Lady Cooper was tired. They had come so far that even he was tired. But she refused to stop.

"I think we'd better—" he said.

"Oh no no no no no no—"

"But we're so tired!" Alex said. "We have to!" And he halted and would not let her go on.

Lady Cooper turned her head away a moment, and when it swung back and she was looking at him she said, "What will, what will, what will—"

"What will?" Alex replied impatiently. "What will what?"

"Become of me?"

"Oh dear," and Alex just stood there, gazing ahead, waiting for her eyes to leave the side of his face. When they did, he steered her in the direction of Rose House.

Keeping his own eyes fixed before him, he said, finally, "I don't know."

Lady Cooper laughed softly and at that moment Alex recognized that the emotion he was feeling was hatred, that a part of him had always believed she was laughing at him, or perhaps at the futility of looking to one such as him.

Neither spoke again until they reached the first road they had crossed. By then they had been walking so long that Alex knew they would have to take that road directly to Rose House rather than go by way of the paths through the forest. It was a narrow, paved road, a winding downhill grade, with eight-foot root-impacted banks instead of shoulders, and there was enough traffic going fast enough to make the walk dangerous. Twice women in Jeep Wagoneers, who assumed that Lady Cooper had escaped and Alex was leading her back, risked accidents to stop and offer lifts.

"No, thank you," he told them and made a little barrier with his smile. He did not want to return to Rose House by car, so visible an admission of irresponsibility. But when the police car stopped, the officer who held the door would not hear Alex's refusal, simply continued to block the way by holding the open door against the embankment until Alex helped Lady Cooper in.

As they pulled away, the one driving said, "The nurse is worried about her."

"I'm sorry," Alex said. "I guess we went too far."

"Don't walk her on the road again."

When they pulled up to the door of Rose House, Nurse Cheam bustled forth with cries of alarm to open Lady Cooper's door and tug at her arm and chastise her for being a naughty girl. Alex got out on the other side.

Stoically the policemen accepted Nurse Cheam's gratitude, declining her offers of hot scones and ice-cold whole milk. After they had pulled away, Nurse Cheam refused Alex's offer to help with Lady Cooper, who was stumbling with fatigue.

One day not a month later, just before Christmas, two men in dark suits from the trust company that administered Lady Cooper's estate came by appointment to see how the Rose Cottage tenant was keeping up the property. The younger man was sparse-bearded, with red eyes, the elder somewhat aquiline, a senior director with burst-blood-vessel British cheeks. Both seemed embarrassed to have to look at how Alex lived. As he was shown through, the senior director commented that he had been to school in England with Lord Cooper, had known him rather well, as a matter of fact.

"How's the writing coming?" he asked Alex.

"Oh, pretty well."

As they were leaving, Alex said, "I wonder if you saw my letter."

"Letter?" replied the senior director, almost eagerly. "Why? Are you giving notice?"

Awkwardly Alex explained no, he'd written to say he was worried that Nurse Cheam was physically abusing Lady Cooper.

To the knowledge of the senior director no such letter had been received. "What evidence do you have?" he wanted to know.

Alex told them about the shouts and the "boxing matches." He did not tell them about Nurse Cheam's throwing off Lady Cooper's bedclothes.

The younger man glanced shyly at Alex. "These are serious charges," he said.

Alex agreed that they were.

The senior director took out his card and wrote something on the back. "You had best write another letter," he said, "to this gentleman."

"I will," Alex said.

And so he wrote again, this time to the indicated gentleman at the trust company.

Towards the end of March he received a letter from the trust company saying that his lease would not be renewed.

Over the next few weeks Alex made visits to health authorities and tenants' rights organizations in an attempt to do something for Lady Cooper and for himself. In the meantime the trust company arranged for two local doctors to examine Lady Cooper. The doctors signed statements declaring no evidence of mistreatment. A legal aid lawyer in a nearby town told Alex that he could do nothing for Lady Cooper, and he took a moment to direct Alex's attention to the wall behind him and the important truth, done by his father in needlepoint, that was framed there: *It's a great life if you don't falter.* But he was willing to help Alex fight his eviction—until he saw the details of the lease. The trust company was pleading something called "discretionary refurbishment," and there was indeed such a clause. Meanwhile Alex's complaint to the trust company must have reached Nurse Cheam, for the offers of icy whole milk ceased. No longer did Nurse Cheam walk Lady Cooper late mornings in the courtyard or the upper garden, only in the lower garden and on the terrace at the south side of the house, where Alex would have been trespassing to go. But on the day before his return to Vancouver, he didn't come back from a walk until nearly seven one evening, and he ran into them in the courtyard.

"Goodbye, Lady Cooper," he said, taking her hand. "My lease hasn't been renewed. I'm going back to Vancouver tomorrow. Goodbye. Thank you. I'll miss you."

But Lady Cooper, whose face was bruised down the left side, only laughed softly and mumbled and did not look at him.

"You'll look after her, won't you, Nurse Cheam?" Alex said, taking her hand too.

"As well as always," Nurse Cheam replied coldly. "It's not easy for anyone. You don't know how she can be."

"No," Alex said. "I see a helpless old woman."

"You don't have to wipe her," Nurse Cheam said.

"No," Alex said. "I don't."

"You don't have to put up with her moods. Day after day. Her childishness. Her cruelty."

"And you don't have to hit her," Alex said.

Here Nurse Cheam drew herself up. "*Don't* you talk to me about what I have to do or don't have to do! How I do my job is none of your business! I am the trained expert here! I see that she gets her meals and her walks and her time on the toilet! Twenty-four hours a day she has me to look after her! I'd like to see you do my job for one week! For one day! You walk with her half an hour when the sun shines, and you think you know what it's like! But you don't! You don't know a single thing about it!"

"You don't have to hit her," Alex said.

And that's when Alex received a punch in the face so quick and hard that he didn't see it coming. But it snapped his head to the right and filled his left eye with tears, and when his vision cleared, Nurse Cheam was walking away with Lady Cooper, who looked back over her shoulder vaguely in Alex's direction, chuckling softly.

That night, Alex's last at Rose Cottage, as he was writing a letter to the senior director suggesting that the trust company hire a home companion to help Nurse Cheam in the afternoons and to allow her at least every other weekend off, smiling to think how these letters to the trust company were the only writing he had done at Rose Cottage, there was a kind of scrabbling at his door, like a branch, or a squirrel, that went on for some time before he went to see what it was, and what it was was Lady Cooper, in a man's green tartan dressing gown and bare feet, coming directly over the threshold, reaching to clutch Alex's hands with cold, strong fingers. Alex tried to step back, but she held him fast. He tried to laugh, he tried to be his gentlemanly self, he tried to be stern, but none of it would come. He made himself return her gaze, but it was difficult, he was afraid it would swallow him.

Her focus was beyond his eyes, on something else. Her wild red face, her murmurous gabble, her brown teeth, she knew him, and the feel of that for him was vertigo. He understood he could fall here, he could fall in. He could let himself go, and then what?

"*So!*" said Nurse Cheam from the doorway, startling them both. "This is where you've come, you naughty, naughty girl!"

"I think she just wanted to say goodbye," Alex said over Lady Cooper's shoulder, though he knew this was untrue.

"Whuh," Lady Cooper said. "*Whuh.*" Her eyes had left him, her fingers let go of his hands.

Nurse Cheam had not remembered to put on her wig. Her hair was thin and grey like an old man's, and her skull looked very strong.

"Well, don't encourage her. Come on, you. It'll be a wonder you haven't caught your death. I can see it's time to start tying you in. Say goodnight to your boyfriend."

"Good night, Lady Cooper," Alex said gently, with sadness and relief. "I'll come back and visit."

But he didn't.

In Vancouver Alex sank back into the person he had been before he left, as if Rose Cottage had not happened. He never seemed to have enough time, always seemed to be doing things too late, scuffling like a dog for a place to live, for enough cab work to keep off welfare but not so much the boredom would kill him. After Rose Cottage the city seemed harsh and raw. When Alex wasn't driving cab he played pick-up basketball at the Y. For some reason he had the idea that if his rooms got enough light he'd have no need for furniture or pictures on the wall. A TV, a mattress, a table to eat at. No curtains. A flower in a vase.

After six months back in Vancouver, Alex was ready to crush the flower. At night he dreamed of Rose Cottage, the paths through the forest by the sea. The next summer he made the trip back. Incredibly it had been almost two years. He told himself that in her condition Lady Cooper would have little sense of the time that had passed. On the walk from the bus stop Alex's life at Rose Cottage came back in force, but the door of Rose House was opened by a small man wearing a white shirt with thick blue stripes and a polkadot bow tie.

"Does Lady Cooper live here?" Alex asked in confusion.

"No, Mummy died," the man replied, looking Alex up and down. "I'm Malcolm. My friends call me Mally. You must be Alex, from the cottage. I love your jacket. Of course, it's leather. I'm making myself a cup of coffee. Won't you join me? I'll catch you up."

Malcolm looked like a younger, softer version of Lord Cooper, whose portrait still hung in the main hall.

"I didn't know you existed," Alex said.

"Call me Mally. I didn't. I was in Italy. You know the sitting room. I'll bring everything through."

The sitting room had been redone. There were Afghan carpets, and the walls were now pale rose. The paintings were suburban watercolours and pastel abstracts. The room was lighter and warmer. Alex crossed to the window to look down the cypress walk and was amazed to see a house not fifteen feet away.

"I *know*," said Mally, wheeling in a tea service. "I had to. Had to turn out old Leadbeater too. He's in a home now. I simply couldn't afford to live here otherwise. Still can't. And I'm a shitty gardener. Cream?"

Mally was an art dealer. Lady Cooper had died six months after Alex returned to Vancouver.

"I appreciate tremendously what you tried to do for Mummy," Mally said. "As soon as I found out, through my spies at the trust co., I had Cheam pensioned off. Looked after Mummy myself. It was horrible. I only did it because I fully expect to be in the same

48

condition one day and I want to be justified when I'm pissed off, and I promise you I will be, because no one's going to lift a fucking finger for me. I mean, Mummy could afford a nurse. Would you mind if I sketched while we talk? You do have the most magnificent mouth—"

Alex did mind, but he said he didn't.

"Just fifteen minutes," Mally promised, moving onto his knees. "It's the line of that marvellous lower lip—"

And so Alex had himself sketched by Mally. The sketching was meant to be preliminary to fellatio. Mally was a good talker, and without saying a thing about it he succeeded in conveying to Alex that there was nothing reciprocal expected, that this would be a forthright no-strings gesture of gratitude for what Alex had tried to do for his mother, and besides, what could be nicer than to return a favour in so delightful a way? Alex would hardly need to put down his cup.

Now, Alex had a long way to go before he could have enjoyed being fellated by a stranger, but mostly his problem was feeling that he hadn't done all that much for Lady Cooper, he should have done more. He felt confused about accepting this favour he neither wanted nor deserved nor considered a favour. Fellatio was something he had allowed women only so that they would indulge his surely incomparably greater desire to witness the fragrance between their legs. But whatever he said as Mally wedged one narrow shoulder and then two between his knees sounded not so much like false modesty as like a running-down conversation in a seduction, when the love-making has already started and the meaning is draining out of the words. Really what Alex wanted to do was jump up.

"Mm, I just love 501s," Mally murmured, his fingers at work on the buttons. The hair on Mally's head was very straight and fine and going a little thin at the top.

Alex could tell that Mally was a gentleman, quite able to chat them through any awkwardness, so that afterwards there would hardly have been an awkwardness at all, whether it was a sudden clamour by Alex to his feet or an uncontrollable bucking of his hips or the tight quick hug and peck on the cheek that he would receive at the door when leaving too quickly (though never quickly enough), and before he knew it he would be on his way across the courtyard and passing through what was left of the roses to step beyond the upper gate and into the forest. Feeling like a pushover, feeling foolish and dismissed and implicated in an unconsidered act of abasement and undoing but otherwise feeling pretty much the way he always felt, pretty much, that is, except for an old small amazement to be so effortlessly, so unaccountably free.

THE
ROARING GIRL

I T WAS 1954, the year the boy turned eight. After dinner he'd
go back to the kitchen for a slice of bread and his parents
would still be at the table with their heads down, talking. If
the boy got too close his mother would grab him and give him a
fierce hug, the way she did when she was drinking. She wasn't
drinking. The boy had been avoiding his father for weeks. He
wanted him, as a man, to solve the problem. He wanted him to do
this before it became necessary to say what it was.

Carefully the boy would separate the crust from the white part
and lower the kinked length of the crust into the garbage pail
under the sink. The white part he'd roll into a ball.

His parents would exchange a look.

One night the boy couldn't take it any more. *"What?"* he
pleaded, squeezing the doughball between his palms.

Slowly his mother turned her eyes from the face of the boy's father to the boy and back to the father. She nodded. The boy's father placed his palms on the table and raised his elbows, tipping
the weight of his torso forward onto his palms. He pushed, and his
body rose. His chair scraped back. The boy watched with care as
his father came towards him. When the man lifted his arm the boy
turned his attention solely to the huge hand, eclipsing the light. It

came down slowly, and then it was pressing the boy's shoulder. The father turned the boy the way he would turn a spigot, and they walked together into the TV room.

The father closed the door. He pointed to the chesterfield. The boy sat on it. The father pulled at the knees of his trousers and squatted in front of him, framing air.

"We didn't want to tell you," he said. "Until we knew for sure."

The boy scraped at the doughball with his teeth. "Tell me what."

"It's your mother."

The boy didn't say anything.

"You remember her appendix burst?"

His mother on this same chesterfield under soaking blankets, her knees pulled up, her face grey and shining. Gritting her teeth. Dr. Mackey had assured her there was nothing wrong, but there was. "When I get something the matter I don't fool around," his mother had said bitterly. And then the ambulance.

"While they were at it," the father said, "they fixed what was wrong down there. Dr. Mackey told her what they'd done, and she just laughed."

He looked at his son with his eyes big, pretending to be amazed at such behaviour, as if the boy was supposed to share this amazement. The boy shifted but otherwise made no response.

The father looked away, towards the window, then back at the boy. "She thought he was kidding."

The boy stared at his father.

The father positioned his hands on his knees and stood up. Looking down at the boy, he said, "So anyway we've been talking about having it, you know, ended. She's too old."

The boy nodded. She seemed old to him.

His father didn't say anything. He was looking at his son.

"So?" the boy said.

"So your mother and I have decided to go ahead. It's a risk, we can't afford it, it'll be hard for everybody, but it's what we're going to do. So if things turn out all right, next year you should have a baby brother. Or sister."

"*What*'s a risk?"

"I told you. Your mother's too old."

The father was back squatting again, running his fingernail along the blond trim of the coffee table. The fingernail had been mutilated. It was yellow and looked braided into the skin.

"The other thing," the father said, watching his finger. Both he and the boy were watching his finger. Machinery where the father worked had mangled it before the boy was born. The enormousness of his father's hands with the marvellous deformed nail, like his father's misshapen stinking feet, were terrible for the boy. He always wanted to touch his father's hands, their size and strength on a whole other scale from his own, but he could never have borne touching his father's feet. "You knew," his father said, "the first one didn't make it?"

No one had told the boy this. He dropped his eyes to the doughball. It was now grey from his hands. All they had ever told him was that he was a miracle. He had assumed they were talking about him.

"She carried it around inside her dead for a long time before anybody knew. She was poisoned. She almost died. You understand what a nervous breakdown is?"

The boy nodded. A failure of the nervous system. The circuits shut down and they put you to bed. Temporary death. Everybody understands.

"When the first one," the father said. "Your mother—If there's trouble this time."

"What kind of trouble?"

"Complications. But we're going to take this thing one day at a time. Trust in medical science, it's a joke, right, but what else can you do? Your mother's a strong woman. I mean physically. By and large. So what do you say?"

"About what?"

"About having a little brother or sister. What the hell do you think we're talking about here?"

The boy shrugged. "Okay, I guess."

His father stood up.

"Let's hope it's okay."

"A boy or girl?" the boy quickly asked. His father was leaving the room.

"That they don't tell you."

"The one who died."

"Boy."

"What was his name?"

The father stopped with his hand on the door and looked around at the boy. "It didn't come to names," he said. "The thing was dead."

"But if it wasn't?"

"Why?"

The boy shrugged.

"Jim," the father said. "If it was a boy we were going to call him Jim."

"That's my name," the boy said.

The father sighed. "That's right. You made it, so you got the name. It's not as if it wasn't like new."

When his father was gone the boy rolled the bread into a harder, rounder, darker ball and took a bite.

———————

The boy had been worried that his mother had a fatal disease, but now that he knew what she had he was no less worried. He simply took on his father's concern. The boy had always worried about his parents. That their presence in the world was tentative he could see in their exceptional physical beauty together with the horror of their feet, his father's broad like a duck's, so high-arched as to appear to be recoiling in repulsion from the earth; his mother's narrow, bony, long and flat, heavily bunioned. His father would remove his socks, and the stench would rise up, driving the boy back, while his mother's feet were absolutely out of bounds to him for reasons of great sensitivity and great pain, which he ascribed to the way she thumped down so hard on them when she walked, in her need to say *Here I come*, as if she too knew her existence was a matter of dispute or uncertainty and required proof. He imagined the misshapen bones inside the shiny veined skin cracked and faulted and jarred out of kilter like boulders submitted to great stress.

After the father had spoken to his son in the TV room, the conversations in the kitchen ceased. Instead he stayed on alone at the table with a ballpoint pen and a pad of lined yellow paper. This was what he did when he was planning to make extra money: an ice-cream concession, miniature golf in a vacant lot, real estate without a licence. None of these schemes had ever come to anything. This time the father worked away until a Friday in March, when he failed to come home for dinner. The boy and his mother ate in silence. The boy was worried, but his mother was merely furious. Three hours later, as she was reading to him, they heard the door. The father came into the boy's bedroom with his eyes bugged-out and glassy, and it was easy for the boy's mother to draw him into a violent argument that passed down the stairs and back and forth through the rooms on the main floor. The boy slipped from his bed and shut himself in his closet where he hummed and sang. After a while the front door slammed and the house was quiet.

The father came up the stairs and walked to the centre of the boy's room. The boy pushed open the door of the closet with his foot. When the door had passed from between them the father was in the darkness swaying a little and breathing heavily as he gazed down at his son. "Your mother's no good with change," he said.

The father was slow to get into the car. By the time he caught up to his wife she was striding down the highway. Years later he told the boy, in the special tone of incredulity he reserved for talking about this woman he had married, that as soon as she saw him coming she hopped a fence and started across a field. He tackled her a hundred yards out, in the stubble—carefully, because she was pregnant—and walked her back to the car. He then drove along the highway a short way and pulled off onto a jetty of fill, to the edge of a pit in front of a small compound with half-built, chest-high walls in concrete block.

The fact of the mud and the pit and the concrete block must have conveyed to the boy's mother the fact that there would be no turning back. By the time he saw her again her eyes were red, but her shoes were heavy with clay and she was smiling. Her initial resistance had been due to her old conviction that service stations, like pool halls and pawn shops, were low, but when she and the boy's father sat across the kitchen table and told him about the station, and his father said they would now have two degrees in the family—BA 88 and 98—his mother laughed. She mentioned the plaque over the door, which would have his father's name on it as proprietor.

"Should have the bank's," his father said.

The service station was under construction on a stretch of two-lane highway that connected the village and a few villages west of it to a four-lane highway. Mostly along either side were fields, but also a trucking depot, a market-garden store, high-tension pylons, a cement factory, and a weedy avocado-coloured motel called the Adventure Motor Lodge. The father, who had foresight, saw the strip as it would become only thirty years later: a six-lane road-town. Plazas, wholesale outlets, a twenty-storey pink-stucco hotel, fast-food places, car lots, subdivisions crowding in from behind.

The father talked a man he knew from the Legion into quitting his job at Hydro to work at the station weekdays from eight to six, because he himself would keep his factory job, at least until the station "got off the ground." Ed Walsh was a handsome duck-tailed drowsy individual who lived with his even drowsier wife, Noreen, on that same stretch of highway, a coincidence that seemed more than anything to dispose him favourably to the enterprise, as if he would naturally want to be involved in anything that happened along there. Though the boy understood that Ed Walsh was to be paid approximately what he had been earning at Hydro, he worried that his father should interfere with the life of a man to the extent of luring him from that kind of security. He tried to talk to his mother about this, but her view that Hydro was too good for Ed Walsh and that his father was paying him at least twice what the job was worth made it a confusing conversation.

The service station opened with a gala on the twenty-fourth of May long weekend: balloons on the pumps, a free plastic tumbler for five gallons or more, a twenty-nine-cent maze game for passengers twelve or under. Many people came, whether they needed gas or not, to wish the father well and to mention how convenient it would be for them to tank up on their way to so-and-so, while the boy fretted that the station should be so raw and unfinished and that his father could not afford to pave even a small area around the pumps. Dust coated everything.

Ed Walsh started Tuesday. Friday evenings and all day Saturday the father and the boy took over. On Sundays the station was closed.

When the boy told him he did not want to work at the service station, the father told the boy it was time he got a taste of the real world. The boy knew his father believed this, but he also knew that mainly he was there to give his mother Saturdays. He was certainly no help to his father. Maybe other kids his age could pump gas without putting in more than the customer asked for; spilling it down the side of the car; leaving the gas cap on the ground, the trunk, the roof; confusing one-dollar bills with twenties. Serving people rattled the boy. He had trouble with the false deference of retail. He would hand customers their change, weeping. Between the conviction that his father was taking unfair advantage and the conviction that unfair advantage was being taken of his father, there was no refuge. Baffled and miserable at the service station, humiliated by his uselessness, dreading the next customer, the next task, anxious about his father's apparent complete lack of automotive know-how, living in fear that a car would limp for repairs that his father had not the faintest idea how to provide, or would get all wrong, the boy spent most of his time in a patch of milkweed out back of the station, on imaginary trips behind the wheel of a rolled Rambler.

In his place to help his father, the boy sent his dead brother Jim. As one who knew death, the first Jim would have felt at home with tools and engines, driveshafts, electrical systems, the smell of dust and exhaust and gasoline and foul toilets. He would have known how to check the oil, change a tire, wind the air hose neatly back on its hook. How to hit the right note with Ed Walsh and the customers in their curlers and their crew cuts, leaning out of their cars with unexpected jokes and remarks. But what it really came down to was, his brother would not have hidden out back.

The very first Friday night the boy and his father arrived to work at the service station the boy had found an empty rye bottle in the waste can by the cash register.

"Guess I better have a word with Ed," his father had said, taking the bottle out of the boy's hand and lowering it back into the can. But if he did have a word with Ed it was not enough even for Ed to bother hiding his empties. Some Fridays there were three. Seagram's Triple Crown.

A couple of weeks later, thieves emptied the till and shat on the desk.

"Why'd they have to shit on the desk?" the father asked the boy.

On Sunday they went to a farm where the man kept dogs in his barn, like short cattle. They bought a German shepherd with the eyes of a shark. During the day the father kept this animal chained to a stake alongside the station. At night it slept on blankets in a corner of the service area. To the boy, owning a dog that was not a pet went with running a service station: a circumstance from another family's life. And he doubted very much that his brother would have agreed their father had done the right thing.

Sooner or later after the boy had got used to a new place, he would catch a glimpse of it the way it looked when he first saw it, and then it was another place altogether, because his entry point of view and the interior point of view that living in it had created were so very different. But in the case of the service station the boy's entry point of view, once it shifted from the highway out front, not only failed to locate itself properly inside the station but split into two: the driver's seat of the rolled Rambler out back, from where he sighted upwards through the missing windshield to the rear of the building on its platform of gravel; and the chair by the cash register in the office, from where his eyes would move from the perceptible creep of the wall-clock minute hand to the window, beyond whose streaked dust was a tar sideroad and a row of flashing money-trees. The interior of the garage itself did not stop being a darkness and a mystery to the boy, and this was the daily world of his brother Jim. At night it belonged to the dog.

One Saturday morning in July as the boy and his father arrived at the station his father said, "Hell." The boy thought he'd forgotten something, but when they pulled up to the office the boy could hear the hoarse bark of the dog from inside. His father told him to wait in the car and keep the doors locked. Now the boy could see what his father had seen: the office doorjamb splintered. He watched his father pass through the office and enter the interior darkness of the service area. He heard him shout the dog quiet.

When the boy got out of the car he thought at first his legs would collapse under him, but they turned out strong, as if they could take him anywhere. Where they took him was to the window slat in the garage door. In order to see through the slat he had to drag over a concrete block and wipe the dust with his sleeve. He could see his father talking down into the grease pit while the dog paced the edge, whining and yearning. The boy slipped into the office, where he sat on the vinyl bench for customers.

"—wish jail on a bank robber," he heard his father say. "Hold on while I get the dog."

The boy crossed to the door with the sign over it that said *Customers Not Allowed Beyond This Point*. His father had one hand on the dog's collar, and the dog kept choking from straining against it. When a canvas sack flipped up out of the pit and crashed on the floor of the garage, the dog scrambled back, yelping, and his father lost his grip. He grabbed for the dog's collar and held it now with both hands. Somebody was climbing out of the pit. The boy went back to his chair. He knew this was not Jim, who was dead, but still he felt responsible, as if this might be his own adversary or shadow or what must happen when his father got in over his head and his son was no use to him.

The girl came into the office carrying the canvas sack, which clanked like aluminum when it grazed the doorjamb. She set the sack on the floor and stood with her arms at her sides, looking at the boy. She was wearing a greasy mud-coloured car coat over a no-longer white T-shirt and dirty pale blue stovepipe jeans. On her feet were ragged running shoes without socks. Her face had an ashen sheen and was covered in small red bites, and her hair had the rat's-nest look of the hair of children at school with lice. Her eyes were starvation-dull, as if she had wasted away inside to something very small and then departed.

"Lyn, this is my son, Jim," the father said, coming into the office, not noticing that the boy was not waiting in the car. The boy was shocked to see that the girl was a half-head taller than his father. It was as if in the dark of the service area his father had been shrunk with a spell.

The girl's eyes closed. When she swayed, the father and the boy both moved to catch her, but the father was on the other side of the desk with his hand on the phone and the boy hesitated. She folded over a corner of the desk and then the boy was there to keep her from the floor until his father came around the desk. She was very light and she stank. Most of her weight seemed to be in the pockets of her coat. The father kicked the sack out of the way and laid her out on the vinyl bench with her knees up because she was too tall. Her face was bloodless and slack. The father did not seem to know what to do. After a few minutes he called Dr. Mackey, who told him to sit her up and give her a little Coke and if that didn't work to bring her in. When the boy came back from the Coke machine his father had the girl sitting up on the bench. She seemed very weak or dazed. The boy was reaching across the cash register for a straw when the phone rang.

It was Dr. Mackey. "Tell your dad, on second thought, bring her in. I honestly don't know what I'm thinking of sometimes."

"Harv change his mind?" the father said as the boy hung up.

With the boy opening the door the father carried the girl to his car, and the boy helped prop her up in the passenger's seat. When the boy got into the back the father twisted around and said, "Where are you going?"

The boy got out of the car and walked through the dust of his father's departure to the office, where he sat in his chair behind the desk and prayed there would be no customers. After a while he looked inside the canvas sack. Hubcaps. He went to the window and looked at the six or seven cars parked around the station. No hubcaps. The bell rang, and he put five dollars' worth of 88 into a

Plymouth. He was so rattled the customer had to come into the office to claim his change. Fifteen minutes later a woman in a pickup wanted her oil checked, but it took her and the boy five minutes to figure out how to open the hood and another ten searching for the dipstick before she gave up and drove away without any word of kindness for him at all. By the time the boy was making change for a man on a motorbike with a tattoo on his forehead, he was having trouble recognizing denominations.

It was noon before the father got back.

"Where is she?" the boy said.

"Resting comfortably."

"Where?"

"Our place."

"Is Mum there?"

"I don't know where your mother is. Out."

His father picked up the phone to order hamburgers.

"Lunch," he said when he hung up. "But first let's get these things back on."

And so they went around the lot trying to guess which hubcaps went on which cars. Only one set was stamped *Ford*, and there were no Fords. "Nobody notices hubcaps," the father said. "Including their own. Unless they're missing. Even then it can take days." When all the hubcaps were on wheels they would fit, the father left again, for the Dairy Bar, to pick up the hamburgers. There were no customers at the station. Upon his father's return the boy's body flooded with relief.

As they ate their hamburgers the boy said, "Why'd she take them off?"

"Because she hasn't eaten in a week."

"Who is she?"

"She's not saying."

"Is she going to be okay?"

"Harv thinks so, but Harv hasn't been right yet."

62

It was like the father not to warn his wife that she would come upon a ragged stranger asleep on their chesterfield. He dialed home once but put down the receiver almost immediately. "Better not wake the kid up."

"Mum'll go crazy," the boy said, but it did not occur to him that his father could have done things differently. It was evident that his father relished the thought of the shock to his wife, and so did he. It would be like a practical joke.

A few hours later the mother called, quiet so as not to be heard but also with the kind of rage the unexpected tended to throw her into.

"It's okay," the father kept saying. "Relax, relax," and, "No, I didn't say how long."

That night when the boy and his father got home, the mother was darting around in an artificial way, telling them things they already knew, for the ears of their guest, who sat on the chesterfield smoking a cigarette with a blanket around her shoulders. When the mother, making dinner, said the girl could have the rec room, the father replied that maybe they ought to move slowly on this, monitor the situation, but the boy could tell he was pleased. To the boy it seemed that his parents' moods dictated their opinions and positions, and for them integrity consisted simply in not forsaking a commitment made in some previous mood. The fact was, his parents would say yes to practically anything, because sooner or later, in one mood or another, they would swing around to yes, and then they would stick to it, defending as natural and right what in the exact same mood two days earlier had been beyond consideration.

The girl came to the kitchen table like a dreamer stumbling into the next dream. She was wearing the father's dressing gown over the mother's nightdress. She was clean and her hair had been washed, though not brushed, or it if had been brushed it was not brushed now. She seemed exhausted, disoriented by the lights. The mother had given instructions to the father and the boy that they were to ask no searching questions. Instead the mother left pauses in her own stream of talk for the girl to fill if she would. The girl would not.

"There's nothing I love more than travel," the mother was saying. "I can stare out the window all day, fall asleep in a motel, jump up first thing in the morning, and do it all the next day and the next and the day after that."

This was true. The mother was rarely happier than as a passenger in a moving vehicle. On long trips she and her husband would drink rye and Coke from a thermos while the boy lay on the back seat reading comic books.

The boy stole a look at the girl to see how she was taking this information about his mother's love of travel. When her expression told him nothing beyond that she was not going to respond, he looked to his mother, whose words through the ears of the girl he found suddenly arcane and foolish. The pauses left by his mother were slight enough to go unfilled without embarrassment. But still. The girl continued to stare at her and not speak. The mother went on talking until, not waiting for a pause, the girl wiped her nose with an upward movement of the back of her hand and said, "Look. I'm fuckin' shattered."

"I'm not surprised!" the mother cried, leaping up, and she and the father helped the girl back to the chesterfield.

While washing the dishes the parents debated in whispers while the boy sat at the kitchen table and listened. He wanted to know if his father would tell his mother about the hubcaps. His father did not. His mother was filled with pity for the girl in her recent misfortune, whatever it was. After a while his father pretended to wipe his nose with an upward movement of the back of his hand and said, "Let's just give her a roof over her fuckin' head until she gets back on her fuckin' feet."

And that is what they did: gave the girl their reç room, a window-less twelve-by-six basement partition in pine paperboard. She didn't seem to mind. Unlike the boy she had no trouble breathing down there, with all the old cat hairs. Just remembering that room can still close the throat of the boy today.

To pay her room and board and for a small wage, the girl, who said she was eighteen but was probably younger, pumped gas Monday to Friday while Ed Walsh worked on the cars. Friday nights and Saturdays she pumped gas while the father, who did not have the energy for two jobs, slept in the office with his feet up on the desk. When she was not on the pumps she was under the cars that Ed Walsh had not got around to during the week. "She's got a real fuckin' knack," said the father, who had still not got over the girl's first words. The boy sat in the rolled Rambler drinking Cokes from the machine.

As far as the boy could tell, his parents made no effort to find out who the girl was, her true age, or what her story was. The father was the kind of man who was a long way from paying taxes and yet who, from the time the necessity of doing so had been impressed upon him, would just hand a big pile of everything over to an accountant. It was like the boy's parents not to want to know more than what came out spontaneously, just as it was like the father, if he paid the girl anything, to pay her from the till. He liked to be in charge, and he liked to do things in a way that felt natural to himself. He liked to take people at their word and in all matters to involve the claims and opinions of as few others as possible. As long as he was curious about the outcome, he enjoyed trusting people because either way, given the roots of his sanguinity in an essential pessimism, he won. To the boy it seemed sometimes that his father arranged the world to conform to specifications for existence inside his own mind.

On the Sunday night following the first week she worked at the service station, the girl finished eating before anyone else and lit a cigarette, which she smoked in silence. After a few minutes she ground it out in her creamed corn, her face pulled back in a kind of smile or grimace that revealed her canines, which in their prominence (the boy had not realized until that moment) were what cancelled her beauty, and said, "Listen, I appreciate what you're doin' for me here, and that's why I'm tellin' you Ed Walsh is useless as a male tit."

At that moment the boy needed to know how to understand the girl in some larger way than his own. He looked to his parents. His father had pushed away his plate with his greasy thumb and turned himself in profile to the table, his left elbow hooked over the back of his chair, his legs crossed at the knees. This meant he was finished eating. He glanced at the girl then away again and went on picking his teeth with a matchbook. The boy could see how embarrassed he was. His mother's smile was so tight she looked as though she had just come from a freezing at the dentist. "Let us worry about Ed Walsh, Lyn," she said. "As long as he doesn't bother you. That's all you need to worry about."

"Bother me? Well, for starters, doin' two jobs fuckin' bothers me."

Later the boy heard his mother tell his father that the girl was jagged around the edges though basically a "good little kid." But his mother always called people she considered inferior *little*, whatever size they were. She called Ed Walsh's wife Noreen *little*, and Noreen weighed two hundred and fifty pounds.

On Saturdays the boy would lie at the edge of the grease pit and watch the girl reach up into the iron undersides of cars, a lightbulb in mesh on a cord hooked up there, her heavy blackened hands sunk to the elbows to perform unknown functions. Sundays after lunch and on Monday to Thursday evenings after her solitary meal, the girl would sit on the back step of the parents' house with a cigarette in one hand and the other upturned in her lap, and the boy would hang around or clamber in the nearest tree pretending to be lost in play, hoping she would acknowledge him. After a few weeks he asked, "What are you doing?"

"Waitin' for you to break your neck."

"What are you thinking about?"

"That's for me to know and you to find out."

"Why don't you go to school?"

"I quit."

"Do you like working at my dad's station?"

"Beats a kick in the ass."

Because the boy understood so little, he wanted to know everything about the girl, and he wanted to know everything that she knew. Her basement room was of tremendous interest to him. Everything she touched, though in origin it was all the family's, was significant to him, the narrow cot, the comb on top of the empty orange dresser, her toothbrush in the chalky family glass on the back of the bathroom sink upstairs. He could hardly believe that as she reached for her toothbrush she witnessed the flying fish decal on the wall under the bathroom mirror, a scene that was part of himself—he had been riding those fish over that decal sea for as long as he could remember—and he wanted to know exactly how she saw them, because he wanted to know in what way it would be possible for himself to be known by her, known completely, like a car she would work on: he wanted to be fixed by her by being known, by being thoroughly and utterly known. The boy's mother was hard-surfaced and fragile and yet capable of great and sudden intimacy that charged the girl's hard surface with promise of a deeper understanding or perhaps lawlessness that he could not understand at all but that drew him like a magnet, like water or the night.

Once as the girl was helping the boy stage wrecks with his model train, she asked him if he knew what a cunt was.

The boy nodded. A flat-bottomed boat you pushed with a pole.

67

"That's where your mum's baby's comin' out," the girl said. "Like a fuckin' fish."

The boy nodded, picturing Baby Moses poling a flat-bottomed basket through bulrushes, headed for the sea, but also sensing that he was being treated like a child, and so he said, "The first one died in her. His name was Jim, too."

"Jesus," the girl said.

Sometimes she would play with the boy, and after a while she would slip into a kind of baby talk, indulging her voice and her laugh, caressing the sounds in a full-throated, teasing way that made the boy uncomfortable. Other times when they were playing, she would become unexpectedly loud and coarse and tormenting, as if she had forgotten who he was, or perhaps that he was there at all, and he would cower in shy dismay, and the cause of so sudden a shift in her nature would be mysterious to him, and in his mind he would go back over and over the course of their play to find it, but he never did.

Now that the parents had a resident baby-sitter they went out after the girl got home from the station on Friday nights as well as on Saturday nights, and she and the boy would play Hearts or Monopoly, him in his pyjamas, and to the boy these occasions promised great intimacy, and he would say and do foolish things, false, willed things, as if it were necessary to extend the range of his nature in order to attract her, or as if it were necessary to demonstrate his willingness for her sake to violate his own integrity, and these things were a long way from what he could be proud of, and yet she would respond, when she responded at all, with neither interest nor scorn nor impatience nor fatigue but simply a flat detachment. But it seemed to the boy that if what he was doing was wrong and even in a way shameful, then why couldn't she see it? Other times he thought: If these things mean nothing to her, then why can't she just know me the way she would do anything else? And he would ask himself, did he still want her to if it didn't mean anything to her? And he would think, yes. And then he would be afraid that she never would.

As soon as the boy had been put to bed, being baby-sat by the girl became a terrible experience for him, because she would turn on the TV and watch it with the sound turned up so loud he couldn't sleep.

One night he jolted awake to crashing music and shouting men. He eased downstairs shaking. A war movie was on. Ships tossing on grey seas, firing big recoil guns. The girl was asleep on the chesterfield. The boy stayed in the kitchen for a long time working up the courage, and then he walked into the living room and turned down the TV.

Foggily, incredulous, from behind him, as if speaking out of some other life, in the comparative quiet, the girl said, "What the fuck are you *doin'*?"

The boy ducked his head and ran for the stairs.

The more time the boy spent with the girl the more attached to her he became but also the more afraid of her. He almost talked to his parents. He could tell from the looks he was getting that they wanted to know what he thought about her. But he couldn't trust them to understand.

One Saturday the boy and his father came home for lunch while the girl covered for them at the station, and his mother put the question to him directly.

He shrugged. "She's okay, I guess."

"She plays with you," his mother said. "She doesn't have to."

"Yeah."

"So what's wrong with her?"

"Nothing. I just don't like her all that much."

This was hardly accurate, but at that moment it was as close as he was able to get. Between what the boy felt and what he was able to say there existed a gap. He would stand and stare out across it and the distance would be the distance between himself and his brother Jim, and he would become more and more afraid, and in the midst of his fear he would hear himself already starting to say the only sort of thing that he was capable of saying. And it would be ridiculous really, and he would know that truth had nothing to do with it at all.

The parents gave each other one of their looks.

The mother asked him why he didn't like the girl.

"I don't like the way she talks."

Another look.

By this time the boy was trembling. He knew that he did not understand his feelings about the girl well enough to have any control over his parents' reactions to what he might tell them.

"What's wrong with the way she talks?" his mother asked.

The boy shrugged.

"Does she use bad language?"

Of course she did. "What do you mean?"

The parents looked at each other.

The father tried again. "Listen, Jim. You're going to find out in this life that not everybody's had the chances you've had."

The boy nodded.

"You don't not like somebody," the father said, "because they don't happen to talk and think the way you do. It's a big world, and there's room for everybody. The sooner you learn that the better."

The boy nodded.

The father looked at the mother.

The family continued eating.

The girl stayed with the family all that summer into the dog days, into the powdery empty space of heat when snakes moved through the milkweed in pairs. The boy would leap back from one snake and another would be rustling away behind him. By noon the sun would heat the interior of the rolled Rambler to 120 degrees, and he would crawl from it to burrow like a dog into the gravel in the margin of shade along the back wall of the station and lie there and wait for the girl. With the heat and no one on the roads, business was slow and there was nothing for her to do once she had made the place as clean and orderly as a kitchen in iron and concrete and gravel and dust, finished all the cars in Service, and even raked the lot, and she would sit out back with the boy while the father slept in the office with fewer interruptions than at home, where his wife in her condition was expecting to be given more help around the house. "She's expecting, all right," the boy heard his father tell a customer.

The girl would come out behind the station and smoke a cigarette with her legs crossed under her and her back flat against the concrete block. Sometimes she would stare out across the rippling fields and sometimes close her eyes. Either way she would not say anything and when the boy spoke—"Is it ever hot, eh?"—jolt like a person falling.

A few times Ed Walsh came around to find her—though years later the boy could never understand why he and Ed Walsh should have been at the station at the same time—and then Walsh and the girl would bicker in such a clipped quick ritual way, so light and abusive, that the boy could not follow it. He would stare at Ed Walsh, wishing with all his heart that he would leave, and he would marvel that the girl could inspire such quickness out of so sluggish a man, and also that they could go on saying such fast sharp things to each other without either of them becoming the least bit upset. They seemed like people who had recovered a kind of complacency in their mutual harshness. On one occasion when they were arguing about something mysterious to the boy, he was relieved to hear the bell at the pumps sound because Ed Walsh would now have to leave, but together they turned on him, and he was the one who had to go and serve the customer.

By that time it was clear that the problems present from the start at the station had evolved but not gone away. The first was that the father could not afford to pay the girl any more than he could afford to pay Ed Walsh. The idea had been that, with the girl on the pumps, Ed Walsh could get more work done in Service, and the extra profits would cover the girl's small salary, but the fact that Ed just drank more was clear from the waste can.

The second problem was the tension between Ed and the girl. Obviously Ed had lost the bossless boozy solitude he had partly taken the job for, while the girl's constant point to the father was that she could run the place by herself for less than what Ed Walsh was being paid to sit in the office and drink all day.

The third problem was that money was disappearing from the till.

By now the mother was enormous and crying a lot. To the boy she seemed more beautiful than ever but tired. The father was just tired. At some point it came to be important to the boy that the girl be gone from among them by the time the baby arrived, but as usual with him the father was reluctant to act, while the mother interpreted any allusion by the boy to the girl's leaving as veiled snobbish harassment of the "poor little kid."

One afternoon the boy was moving like a hunter through the girl's room, seeking to cool the fever of this person in his mind, but what he found, in her bottom drawer, was a magazine filled with colour photographs of women lying mostly on their backs, though a few had chosen their stomachs, spreading their legs, with their high heels high in the air, some with men standing or kneeling with closed eyes and sneering or perhaps snarling faces and broad right-angled penises engulfed by the women's bodies, and these pictures cooled him not at all. The boy was so shocked by the women's hairiness and the raw pink redness like a mutilation, by the worn soles of their high heels, but mostly by the way one of them twisted around to look straight out at him, as if to defy him to expect her to be ashamed, that almost as soon as he looked at those pictures his stomach hurt. He put the magazine back in the drawer and crept from the room like an animal that has received a physical blow.

The girl did not discover him that first time, but the magazine was too rich, that was all. It seemed to require small doses, little peeks, like an old man's snorts from a hidden bottle. And then bolder and more careless, until, *"You fuckin' little sneak—"*

Later that night she pinned him on the stairs. "Listen," she said quietly. "It's nothin'. Dirty old Ed's got stacks. But you tell and so help me I'll break your fuckin' legs."

The next night Noreen Walsh called to ask where Ed was. The father said he knew they were gone as soon as he saw the till empty, but the boy knew already. When his father turned apologetically from the empty till and said, "This part wouldn't have been Ed's idea, you know," the boy nodded. When his father said later it was easily worth a week's income to be rid of those two, the boy nodded again, but he also thought this was just something his father would say to make it seem like a convenience that he had been robbed again.

A week later the boy had a little brother, Wayne, seven pounds, fourteen ounces. Wayne was a sickly baby, and his crying irritated the boy. Maybe if babies could measure up to the dead. Maybe if you could understand what they wanted. Maybe if they could talk. A few weeks after that the father was fired from his job at the factory for a screw-thread contract he fumbled in his fatigue, and a month later he walked away from the service station because it was his salary from the factory he had been using to keep it going. Walked away and went on unemployment. Paid the man with the dog barn to take back the German shepherd.

The mother found work as a bookkeeper.

A few months later, while Wayne was napping, the father was vacuuming around the boy's bed when he found the magazine.

"What's this?" he said, holding it in the air as he came into the living room where the boy was playing with his plastic men.

The boy looked up. "It was in her room," he said. "I think it was Ed Walsh's." The boy said this before he knew that he would. For some reason he wanted to protect the girl. He also wanted to be helpful here. He was very frightened. That this was an inevitable moment he knew from the way his mind had travelled outside it to make so many versions even as it was happening.

"You don't want to look at crap like this," the father said. He was wearing the big workshop apron he wore when he housecleaned.

"Not really," the boy said, and fought to keep his eyes up, meeting his father's.

The father left the room. The boy heard him put the magazine in the garbage under the sink, then take the bag to the outside pail. When the father came back he reappeared at the door. "If I were you," he said, "I wouldn't tell your mother."

The boy nodded.

All his adult life the boy will have a memory—and it will be imbued with that aura-vividness of life outside habit—of walking down the street with the girl. He had never walked with her before, he had never gone anywhere alone with her. He will never remember where they were going or what they did there, but he will remember her scuffed pumps flashing out from under the hem of the cotton dress, her narrow torso balanced on the moving fulcrum of her gait, her large hands at her sides, scrubbed clean, her face remote and empty, and when, rarely, the eyes from their great height turned downward to him as she spoke, the pocky jawline, the protuberant canines when she laughed, the brown weight of the hair fallen forward, he will not know who this was, will remember only his amazement at the time that they should be moving along at the same pace, that he should be contained in any form at all within that alien, unconscionable mind. And his heart will just roar.

THE AGE
OF REASON

I F AUDREY HAINS eats later than she's used to she gets a migraine, so this time Stan promised her eight o'clock absolutely and without fail. Meaning that as soon as Stan's wife Cynthia started in on the whole thing of figuring out what to wear, having a bath, putting pyjamas on their son Shane, brushing Shane's teeth, getting Shane to choose a book for his bedtime read, etc., etc., Stan right away tidied the rec room, ironed a shirt, got dressed, and drove over to pick up the baby-sitter, whose name was Harriet.

As he parked in front of Harriet's house, Stan could see the back of her head in the picture window. Two ponytails. She was watching TV, all ready to go.

"Bye, Mumm-o," Harriet called to her mother as she came out to the step where Stan waited.

In his car Stan had *Graceland* on the tape deck, and he bet Harriet her mother would like it, if she didn't know it already. A few months ago Harriet had revealed that her mother, a six-foot woman with a strong Norwegian accent, loved The Crystals, and Stan had not been able to forget this. Harriet had never heard of *Graceland*, though she had seen Paul Simon once, on "The Muppet Show." At Stan's place they sat in the back lane for a bit while she studied the picture of the medieval figure on the cassette cover. She thought it was neat. Stan told her it was from the Bayeux Tapestry.

A few minutes later, as he walked around waving his arms to get the movement-sensitive light over the back gate to come on, he thought, How do I know?

Inside it was twenty to eight and Cynthia was still reading to Shane. Stan got the intercom organized, found a paper bag for the wine, wrote down Charles and Audrey's number, and took Harriet in to say goodnight to Shane, who said "G'night" in a flat voice with his face turned to the wall. Then Harriet and Stan stood by uncomfortably while Shane and Cynthia went into their final routine.

"First Mummy's going to finish putting on her make-up, and then she's going to go out for dinner with Dad but not for too long, and then she'll come home and snuffle snuffle snuffle until she hears her sweetest little angel in the whole wide world saying *Mummy I'm cold* or *Mummy I had a bad dream* or *Mummy I'm wet* or *Mummy come and cuddle* or *Mummy I want to get up...*"

Shane put his arms around Cynthia's neck and whispered, "Mummy, if you can't go, please don't."

And Cynthia laughed and extricated herself. "But I can and I have to."

"I'm not worried too much," Shane said to the ceiling as Cynthia left the room.

"That's good, sweetie," she called from the bathroom.

"You don't have to worry at all, Shane," Stan said. "Mum and Dad'll be fine."

Shane worried constantly that his mother would break her leg falling down stairs or die in a car accident. He didn't seem to worry about what would happen to Stan, but Stan felt he ought to assume his son worried about both his parents.

"We're just going to some people's for dinner, Shane," Stan

said. "And then we'll come right back. Okay? Goodnight."

Shane's answer was two singsong grunts. He had turned away again.

As he waited for Cynthia to finish putting on her make-up, Stan leaned against the kitchen counter. Harriet sat at the table and told him about Murderball. The boys at school played it in a space divided off by a portable wall. The girls would be sitting in French class and WHAM! the whole wall would bow in maybe three inches.

And that was it, Cynthia, who had gone overboard on the Ombre Rose, was all ready to go, the usual instructions were said to Harriet, the usual goodbyes to Shane, the usual ardent *Goodbye Mummy*s by him, and they were out the door.

———

Everything was easier in the summer. Everybody was out of the city, so there wasn't even much traffic. The Hainses lived west of the escarpment in a split-level they had picked up from a ruined architect. Stan and Cynthia got there at exactly seventeen minutes past the time Stan had promised and took another two minutes to admire the lawn, if that is the word for buffalo grass and roses.

Inside, the first thing that happened to Stan after he got his shoes off was a big hug from Charles that reminded him how little he knew the man. Stan had no idea how much pressure to return.

Audrey was a colleague of Stan's at the university, and Charles was her husband, some kind of surgeon. For a long time Stan had had trouble identifying the feeling Audrey evoked in him, and then he realized it was fear. Nobody rattled him like Audrey Hains. He was reminded of this when he noticed a book in his hand as Audrey led him and Cynthia towards the living room. He must have picked it up in the hall. What was he thinking of? He glanced back at Charles, who was close behind. Charles' expression seemed to indicate that he should feel free to examine the book, but maybe it didn't. The book was called *The Family Game*, and it appeared to be pop psychology.

The living room had been redone. It could have been a White Sale, milk and silk. Stan recognized the look it was getting from Cynthia: Very nice but D.I.N.K. to the cornices. And then she too was noticing the book in his hand.

"What's that?" she asked.

"That's mine," Audrey said.

Stan passed the book to Cynthia, who knew it from a review in *Vogue*. As Stan's hand went out, he sincerely wished his wife would not dye her hair copper.

To Audrey Cynthia said, "Why are you reading this?"

It must have been the way Cynthia came down on the *you* and the *this*, plus her and Stan's rich history of saying the wrong thing to the Hainses—like the time Charles said, "I suppose you people will think we're pretty bourgeois," and Stan replied, "No, really, it's nice for a change"—that caused Audrey to lean towards Cynthia with her fists on her knees and her teeth clenched and say, "*Don't get me started.*"

She had to be joking of course, but there was something else, and Cynthia dropped the book onto the cushion beside her in mock alarm.

Audrey settled a little in her chair and told them in a casual way that one of her graduate students had given her the book, and she supposed she should read it. Flicking a speck from her shoulder, she added that her mother had died last week, and she hadn't gone to the funeral.

Stan and Cynthia looked at her.

"Where did your mother live?" Stan tried, after a silence.

"It wasn't the drive."

Charles came in with a scarlet and blue lacquered tray in the shape of a parrot; the tray held four martinis.

Stan and Cynthia looked at the martinis.

"A few days ago," Audrey said, "my student told me I seemed distracted, so we talked, and the next day he gave me that book."

"Cheers," said Charles and raised his glass, somewhat grimly, Stan thought.

Neither Cynthia nor Stan had tasted a martini in at least ten years.

"Is your father alive?" Stan asked Audrey cautiously.

"I wouldn't have gone anyway."

"Come on, Aud," Charles said. "It wasn't that easy at the."

Charles' sentences seemed to break off as soon as he knew how they would end.

"We have retired friends," Audrey was saying with amazement. "Actual retired friends. I mean good friends."

"I know," Cynthia said. "Isn't it bizarre."

Stan looked at her and at Audrey.

"People my parents' age," Audrey said to Stan and then seemed to wait, as if he should say something.

"Actually." Charles cleared his throat. "Dave retired at fifty-seven."

"The point is—" Audrey was smoothing her skirt across her knees—"we spent the evening of the day with them. I talked about it, and that helped. I think they understood."

"Regna cried for both of you," Charles said.

"I don't think I know anything about your parents," Stan said to Audrey.

"That's just as well, because I've never talked about them to you."

"Audrey's mother," Charles said and sighed.

"Charles, I don't want to talk about this. I really don't."

"I've got a psychologist friend," Stan said, coming forward to the edge of the sofa so quickly that his pants went tight at the knees. "He says the ones he knows are going to be hard and take a long time and probably never get anywhere at all are the ones who insist they had a happy childhood."

"A psychologist would say something like that," said Cynthia, who considered psychology a racket.

"My brother says our childhood was fine," Audrey said. "He doesn't insist at all."

"Your brother, Audrey," Charles said, "is not exactly an undefended character."

"I don't want to talk about my brother."

"These are unhappy people," Charles said, turning to Stan. He meant the ones who go to psychologists. "It doesn't say others don't have a perfectly. Who'd like a martini?"

"We've had *a* martini," Audrey said. "Why do men think a gentleman is supposed to pretend to have no memory?"

"The big question," Stan said, raising his voice so Charles could hear him from the kitchen, "is, do the people who don't have enormous, life-long, unsolvable problems, who only worry about paying off the mortgage, or how the kids are doing at school, or if their wife still loves them because they sure as heck still love her, do these people actually exist?"

"Cut it out, Stan," Cynthia said.

Stan wondered why Cynthia was so hard on him in public when at home they got along pretty well.

"Once when I was five or six," Charles said, coming back with the drinks, "my father told me if I jumped off the ledge I was standing on, he'd catch me. So I jumped, and he didn't make a move. When I stopped crying, he said, 'Now you know. Never trust anybody'."

"People only have to be themselves to be monsters," Cynthia said.

"And then there's transgression," Audrey said.

"There is," Stan agreed, a little too eagerly but remembering to tug his pants at the knees. "There's your basic egocentrism, more or less a wall, and then there's over-the-wall. The co-ordinates shift, nothing could be easier, you're you and you're not you, and it's great. Except of course to—"

"The victim," Audrey said.

"Well, yes," Stan admitted. "Or society, who may or may not lock you up. Whereas—" he did a big disclaiming shrug—"you were just being not-yourself!"

"What the hell are you talking about?" Cynthia said.

"People."

"People schmeople."

"He means once you put aside integrity," Audrey said, "the rest is a piece of cake."

"Didn't somebody on TV say that?" Stan said.

"Drink up, folks," Charles announced. "Time to choke down."

Charles was one of those surgeons who relax after a hard day in the operating theatre by cooking a gourmet meal. He'd done a brilliant spinach and sweet pepper salad. He'd done salmon on the barbecue, a perfect béarnaise, fresh chervil. Asparagus with pine nuts. Marinated potatoes. There was a good French wine, not the California stuff Stan and Cynthia had brought.

"I think the real question," Cynthia said, examining the piece of salmon on the end of her fork, "is how on earth did we make it? How did we get through at all?"

"Delusion," Stan said.

"I mean—shut up, Stan. What do I mean? I mean, we can relate, more or less."

"Less," Stan said.

"We're not—" Cynthia hesitated.

Charles looked at Audrey. "Cynthia's saying we're not like your brother."

"Make it, not make it," Stan said. "Who's to say, even in hindsight? Listen. Ever since I can remember, my mother used to fly into these unpredictable rages."

"Your mother was destroyed by cortisone," Cynthia said.

"Did I know that at age four, or five? All I learned was how to fly into unpredictable rages."

"You pity her."

"Sure, but it took me half my life to get that far. Meanwhile, already my son hates me."

"No, he doesn't."

"And *your* father—" prompting.

"My father," Cynthia said, dropping her eyes and speaking deliberately, "never got past the war. He used to think I was trying to poison him with my perfume. To this day I carry the mark of old Barry's insane conviction that his daughter was trying to poison him with her perfume." And Cynthia displayed the back of her hand: four little holes, from a table fork.

"Now she's trying to poison me," Stan said, pretending to choke. When nobody laughed, Stan looked at Charles, who had leaned forward to see Cynthia's hand. "Charles," Stan said.

"One night we arrived at the cottage with my father," Charles said, straightening, "and my mother's purse and shoes and dress and half a bottle of vodka were on the dock. She was underneath. She'd gone for a swim and hit her head, but we didn't know. My father put us to bed as if everything was fine. The next morning we stood at the window and watched them pull her out."

Cynthia's hand went to her face.

Stan turned to Audrey.

"My mother used to make me do things," she said.

"What kinds of things?" Stan asked.

"The point is not being loved or not loved," Audrey said, looking straight back at Stan. "Love takes too many forms. The point is, how much can you understand, when. What can you distinguish from what, when." Audrey relaxed a little in her chair. "It's reason, in other words, the God within the mind. 'This light and darkness in our chaos joined, / What shall divide? The God within the mind.'"

"What kinds of things?" Stan said.

Audrey just looked at him. At first he thought her eyes were filling with tears, but it was not that.

"Don't answer him," Cynthia said.

Audrey had no intention of answering him.

———

Stan and Cynthia got back too early for Harriet, who was ten minutes from the end of their *Raising Arizona* tape. Harriet had already seen it twenty-six times and didn't complain. Not that she would have. On the drive over to her place, she talked to Stan about Hallowe'en. She was planning to go door-to-door as Ed Broadbent.

On the way back from dropping off Harriet, Stan listened to *Graceland* turned up very loud.

Around one o'clock Stan and Cynthia were making love when Shane woke with a bad dream. Cynthia was tied to the bedposts, so Stan threw a dressing gown over what he was wearing and went instead. *You come, I'll go*, as the old new-parent joke has it, but you'd think Stan was straight out of that dream. Shane cried louder, for his mother, so Stan had to go back and untie her.

RAT WITH
TANGERINE

T HE IDEA is to get from under the covers to the TV with a
minimum of complication. The idea is to have the grey
winter sunlight closed out. The idea is to keep the morning's last dream rolling like a tangerine around the periphery of the
long, quiet day.

The second quarter is over. In a prerecorded interview the coach
is saying, "We're working as a team now. We're really going out
there together and hurting people."

Bill, watching this, hears the staple gun from the basement.
His son, Adrian, is building again. *Shut the door, it's like gunshots*,
Bill beams at Adrian, who beams back, *Okay, Dad*. But nothing
happens. Results so far on Bill's telepathic career have been inconclusive.

Shortly into the third quarter Diane comes in to fling open the
drapes. *No*, Bill beams, pushing his glasses up his nose, clearing his
throat. Diane shrugs and returns to the kitchen. Hardly telepathy,
maybe, but conflict averted.

After the game one of those educational shows.

"Hey, Adrian!" Bill calls from the top of the cellar stairs. "Come
see this!"

Adrian emerges and joins Bill to watch a chimp talk American sign language with a female psychologist in dark glasses. They're having a conversation, with subtitles.

Who is this? the chimp signs, pointing with a limp hand at the show's host.

"A friend," replies the psychologist.

The chimp makes sarcastic kissing motions at the host, then signs, *When time eat?*

"What do you think, Ben?" the psychologist replies.

Ben is uncertain, the chimp signs. *When time eat?*

During the commercial, Bill turns to Adrian. "I thought language was supposed to make all the difference."

Adrian shrugs.

"Time to redouble efforts on the telepathy," Bill says.

"That's where they've really got you beat."

Bill is gazing at the ceiling.

"There's always gratitude," Adrian says.

"I just want to say how much, Ad, I appreciate your willingness here to—"

Adrian stands up.

"Before you disappear, where's your mother?"

"Primaling."

"See what I mean?"

Adrian seems worried, as if he has something to say, but he goes back to the basement.

Bill walks over and opens the drapes. Across the street and down a bit there is a house he has never seen before. These new developments are really something. Bill walks back to the TV and watches an old Mary Tyler Moore, then a drama about a student nurse. Bill gets a beer and wanders downstairs to visit Adrian, who is stapling chicken wire to a rhomboid frame. Bill stands there with the beer in his hand. Adrian is the first to speak.

"Bad news."

"Shoot." Bill takes a big, staring swig. His last dream is just there at the periphery, a rolling tangerine.

"Wilson died last night." Adrian is working away twisting chicken wire with pliers. "He's the last rat, Dad. It doesn't look good."

"Certain diets can kill?" Bill tries.

"Not so simple. They all lived long and apparently healthy lives. But when I dissected, the ones that could eat whatever they wanted, the ones who got really big and sleek and strong, were the worst diseased. And they all ate different combinations of things."

Bill tries again. "Not wise to offer a rat a wide food choice?"

Adrian is running his fingers along the edge of a spruce slat as if he would like a splinter. "Why not, would you say?"

"You got me," and Bill is thinking, Wouldn't it be nice to just crawl back under the covers and hello dreamland.

"I was thinking about 'disease'," Adrian is saying, "like *dis*ease, you know? I mean, if you consider what it's like for an *animal* to get its food and shelter all taken care of *and* spend its life looking at four walls—"

"I wouldn't put it that way, Ad. You kept them busy enough. That fabulous treadmill you built. Those guys had nothing to complain about. Maybe a little itchiness in the bones, but that's understandable, cooped up all day—"

"It's okay, Dad."

Bill goes back upstairs. He is feeling anxious. Halfway through the second period of a hockey game, a great desire comes over him for one of Diane's bread puddings. He beams *bread pudding* to her at her primal therapy group, or wherever she is. When the game is over he wanders into the kitchen and pokes around in the cupboards, but there is nothing exciting. Diane shops by pure habit, the smallest sizes. Five or six jars of the same thing. Two or three host fungi. Bill checks the sink for the roast that he has hoped will be thawing, but there is nothing. He wanders downstairs to the freezer for pork chops. On his way back he sticks his head in the workshop door but can't think of anything to say. He gazes at the pork chops, hefts them.

"Pork chops," he says.

Adrian nods.

Next there's a Victor Mature movie. Lotsa savanna. Bill is asleep in front of it when he hears the back door and voices. Diane has a full-throated way of talking at times as if her ego is lodged there. Bill tiptoes into the kitchen not wanting to see who is doing this to her voice. He sits down at the kitchen table and beams *bread pudding* as hard as he can.

An ordinary man's head with a fading smile goes past the kitchen window on its way down the back steps. Diane comes into the kitchen and she is still smiling.

———

At dinner Adrian talks about his plans. One is an experiment concerning the effects of different kinds of music on the daily life of caged mice.

Bill suggests he make that the effects of TV on the daily life of caged mice.

"Irradiation study?" Adrian asks. "Cats who sleep on computer terminals get cancer?"

"Sure, and the colour of the light. Diane, tell Adrian what the guy at the party told you about the hookers."

"What guy?" Diane has not been listening. "You tell him."

So Bill explains how big city hotels put blue lights outside to keep prostitutes away because they look like death under them. "Whereas everybody looks terrific under red. Hence red light district, get it? Same with food. People can't eat blue food. Put blue icing on part of a cake and people won't eat that part. Once I put blue food colouring in a guy's baked beans and he just about went insane."

"What about blueberries?" asks Adrian, who is good at scepticism. "What about blue Popsicles?"

"Blueberries are purple," Bill says. "Kids are different. Kids know eating blue drives their parents crazy." But now he's not so sure. Blueberries have reminded him of raisins and raisins of the bread pudding that Diane has not felt like making. The tangerine is there too. "The point about TV," he says, "it sheds a sort of blue-white light. It's a blue world—"

"Maybe TV helps people feel they're back in the sea," Adrian suggests.

"I never thought of that."

"You watch TV all the time," Diane reminds Bill.

"I know." He is the first to admit it. "I just might stop completely. I'm almost drowned." He tells Diane about the chimp talking sign language.

"So what are you saying, Pop?" from Adrian.

"Who knows? I'm brainstorming here. Diane, do you remember what I did after Adrian was born?"

"You went out into the hospital parking lot and howled at the moon. I was never so embarrassed."

"That's right, and I wasn't even self-conscious. Boy, those were the days."

"At least you didn't eat the placenta," Diane says.

"I was thinking of eating the placenta," Bill acknowledges to Adrian, who places his hand over his eyes. "You know, frying it up." Bill pauses a moment then continues. "In the drugstore the other day I overheard a conversation. One guy wanted medicine from the shelf and another guy was explaining how you can tell the quality by picking up vibrations from the packages. All you have to do is hold the different brands in your hands for a few minutes."

"The guy was a screwball," Diane says.

"There are more things in heaven and earth, Di."

89

Adrian is tapping his teeth with his fork. "What's your point, Dad?"

"The rats, son. Tell your mother about the rats." Bill is on his feet circling the table, smacking his fist into his palm. "Diane, don't start doing the dishes. Why do you always start doing the dishes? Stay seated and listen to this."

"You can both talk to me while you're drying."

Adrian explains again about the rats while drying. Bill helps too, then sits on a kitchen chair with his elbows on his knees and his face in his hands. The dishtowel is damp on his shoulder.

As soon as Adrian has finished explaining, Diane says, "People aren't rats."

"True, but they're mammals," Adrian replies.

"Well, they're not rodents."

Adrian and his mother have one of their instant bitter arguments.

Bill sits with his head in his hands. His fingers are pressing into his eyes and making little suns for all the world like blazing tanger—"That's enough, you two."

"You heard your father! *That's enough!*"

Fastidious as a maniac, Adrian is smoothing and squaring his wet dishtowel along the oven door handle. When Bill looks again he is not there. A door slams.

Diane remains at the sink scouring, and Bill sits watching the muscles in the back of her neck. Which he loves. He loves her neck. The muscles in her neck. He means to get up and go on drying but instead he asks her about Mr. Fading Smile, what she intends to do. She shakes her head, lowers herself carefully into the chair across the kitchen table, doesn't know, really. The guy's married, two kids, one an epileptic, and so on. As she talks she seems to become more and more confused, as if the guy has sounded more and more ordinary in the telling. They go over it, and over it. By midnight Diane has gone to bed, and the house is still.

Bill goes down to the basement and offers Adrian, who is shaping a water trough out of tin with pliers, use of the TV for his next experiment. Adrian accepts. Bill asks Adrian what he thinks about open marriage, assuming (he assures him) the situation isn't completely out of control. Not much, judging from Adrian's embarrassed shrug, but kids are notoriously conservative. Bill and Adrian carry the TV downstairs. After that Bill walks around the house switching off lights, locking doors, turning down the thermostat. There is an ugly gap where the TV used to be. Maybe Diane will do something about it. Maybe she won't. Bill opens the drapes and stands in the darkened living room looking out at the cold blue fluorescence of the street. A picture window is just a big screen. It's snowing again. Out there is the sea. Out there it has always been the sea. And Bill goes to bed, curling his body to an S to fit Diane's, and falls asleep and dreams about a cold wind, the front door slamming open, darkness, out of the darkness a white rat walking on hind legs down the hall to the bedroom, tangerine held high in thin ecstatic paws.

A NIGHT
AT THE PALACE

O NE DAY I opened my door and it was Harris. He hadn't knocked. I was on my way out for a chocolate bar. I needed chocolate. Once when I was a kid I picked up the phone to call my father and my father was right there. I hadn't dialled.

"Henry?" my father said.

It was like that. After twenty-five years I wasn't expecting Harris, but after twenty-five years the shock exploded all question of expectation.

When I first saw him again, Harris was still moving towards my door. The hair on his head was no longer ash-blond, it was the colour of ashes, and it poked out the expansion gap in the back of his cap, as I saw when he folded me in his arms.

"Dry those tears," Harris said.

I invited him in.

Harris took the stairs two at a time. I remounted more slowly. In those days I was still living over the TV Repair. An old TV will be filled with roaches like a horse with Greeks. With Harris back I kicked myself for dragging my feet in the accommodation department.

"Where did life go?" I asked him in the kitchen.

"Life's not gone yet," Harris replied. He held up two mickeys of Sauza Gold, one from each pocket of his windbreaker, which was raw silk in green and chartreuse. His jeans protruded with limes.

We sat across from each other at the kitchen table and slammed tequila while Harris told me what he'd been up to: deep-sea rig management in the Tropics of Cancer and Capricorn. Eighty-one sixty-day twenty-four-hour contracts. Descending a ladder for naps in his launch. Between contracts, a small plane into India, buying gold. Seventeen years of this and Harris had married an Englishwoman named Sam and settled down. Built a house in Dominica, and that was all fine.

Later we went to a bar.

At the bar a darker story emerged. Dominica was not the paradise it seems. In other developments, Sam had filed for divorce, while from Colombia two and three death threats a week were showing up on the fax. The atmosphere was poisonous, and Harris had turned inward, to art—he was not, he confessed, a bad painter—and to books, in particular the prophets: Elijah, Revelations, Cayce, Cohen. It was William Blake who said the Road of Excess leads to the Palace of Wisdom.

"That's the road I'm on now," he told me. "I've swung by for you."

This was an old pattern for us. When I was a child, Harris's family would pass by our humble house on their way to church in their late-model Oldsmobile v-8 convertible, Dr. Harris in a double-breasted suit, his beautiful wife frail on the seat beside him, Harris and his sisters in the back seat. I say pass by, but soon after Harris saved my life, they were stopping for me, and however reluctant I might have been to attend church, I would squeeze in beside Mrs. Harris, who smelled of hospitals and lavender talcum, and I learned that being saved is not an event, it is a condition.

"I'm taking you with me," Harris said again now, his voice resonant.

The plan was, we would start out by throwing ourselves into acts of excess at the rural home of Harris's in-laws, who were out of the country until Monday. Later we would travel to distant lands and do the same there. We would be wise before we knew it. Palace regulars.

"Summers are slow at the bookstore," I said, pretending to weigh my decision, my heart slamming. "Jan—she's my boss—would never admit it, but she'll be relieved I'm gone. Why me?"

"You're drowning again, and I love you."

The next morning a call woke me. "This is Glorie from VISA. Sir, what is the name on your card?"

I thought, My God, I've won air miles. Harris is back one day and look at me. "Henry Stetmeyer. That's S-T—"

Glorie laughed a silvery laugh. "I don't think so, sir! Sir? Could you please look at your actual card?"

I told Glorie about an infestation of roaches I had recently suffered in my phone. I was holding it upside-down in my lap, taking it apart with a screwdriver, intending to flush them out, when suddenly from my lap an operator's voice said, "What do you think you're doing?"

"This is a little bit like that," I told Glorie.

Glorie asked if I had looked at my card yet.

It was in my wallet, which all being well was in my pants. My pants were caught on the hall door. With my foot, as I told Glorie about the roaches, I was dragging my pants back to the couch, where I sleep.

Soon I read out the name on my card. *Julia Drake.*

"Right," and Glorie got down to business. I kept saying, Yeah, yeah, uh-huh, but I didn't understand, I was very confused, I wasn't taking in her words. I wanted to know more about this Julia Drake, and then Glorie said, "So is everything clear?" and I said,

"Yeah," and she said, "Thanks for shopping with VISA," and hung up.

I spent the next little while bending my Julia Drake card back and forth until it broke into two pieces. I had caught that much.

As kids Harris and I lived on the same street in different worlds. This was back East. From my bedroom window through the skeleton trees I could see the steel factory, concrete block, half a mile long, my father sleepwalking home. At night in bed I could hear the shift whistles. Harris could hear them too, but for him they sounded from another planet. Harris lived beyond the pavement, in a white frame house at the far, bluff edge of five acres of blue-green grass. From Harris's bedroom window you looked down at a goldfish fountain in a flagstone patio, and then you looked out over the beautiful Falloon Valley.

It was not so much that the Harrises were rich as that I could not reconcile their order of reality with my own. My parents were always right there on the line for me, but I thought I had to choose and I chose the Harrises. Was this for the same reason the most artful depictions are the most convincing? The most insane leaders the most magnetic? Was this because my parents were failures in the eyes of the world? Or was it because my life had been saved by Bruce Harris? Whatever it was, I have never to my knowledge dreamed my parents' house, whereas the Harris house I have been dreaming since I was seven. I was never at home there, I was off-centre and confused on those premises, but I am back there every night, and when I die I will haunt them. When the Harris house is levelled for a Valleyview Estates or a Green Ridge Homes, I will haunt the construction site, I will infest every ticky-tack townhouse.

———————

Lydia I didn't know any more than I knew Julia Drake, but Harris had me picking her up at noon in my old Luxus, to take her to the rural home of his in-laws for some of that excess. A double date. Except I lived downtown, and Lydia at the western limit of all development. Maybe it was a summer Saturday and traffic was light, but still it took me over an hour to get out there.

A prairie day. The same big gusts scooping the grain beyond the service road were shifting and distorting all sounds in the cul-de-sac where Lydia lived. Sprinkler pulses, snatches of radio, bawling children, people calling lawn to lawn. A guy in monster white sneakers was out washing his monster-tire 4-Runner with the doors spread like a beetle's wings, a bottle of beer on the hood, the speakers pounding. On one doorstep four teenagers with dyed half-haircuts sprawled with their blaster. A toddler kept screaming and falling as it tried to manoeuvre an over-sized plastic-wheeled tricycle on the new sod.

A girl possibly twelve or thirteen was sitting splay-legged in the driveway of the house with the number I was after. I parked in the street.

From the front walk I said Hi to the girl in the driveway.

She was sucking her thumb. Her legs were thin and bug-bitten. With her free hand she scratched her hip under her dress as she turned to watch me.

Everything here was pristine and chemical. The fragrance of tar and fresh cement. Silicone and vinyl. The concrete front stoop under me was very smooth and it resonated like a drum.

I rang the bell. After a while the clicking steel tumble of pins and then the wham of a hollow door on a chain when it jolts rigid.

"Hi, you look terrible. I'm on the phone."

It was too bright out to see her face, but her teeth gleamed. The crack narrowed, the chain slid and fell, swinging. The door opened.

"I know, I was out drink—" but already she was down the parquet, the phone in the crook of her neck, sweeping the cord like a lounge singer. Later I noticed it was a cordless phone. She was wearing black leggings and a green shirt.

To the person on the phone she was explaining how much somebody named Dieter hated pretension. "He always hated it in me and of course in himself. He hated anybody, really, who tried to rise above. Hated them enough to kill them. I'm serious."

"Pour yourself a drink," she mouthed as she came back towards me and cut left into a room that echoed. "But he was so creative. In Seattle? He hand-painted our own frieze, around the bedroom ceiling. Thirty-six scenes, nine a side. They said everything there is to say. It was, now I know. This was his Mandrax period. I stopped counting the number of times he fell off that ladder. Listen, I have to go."

She was a small person, possibly five-four, a tight package. She wore her hair cropped and black, and in her eyes was the kind of rage that I have been finding more and more attractive in a woman. She was probably my age, forty.

"Dieter," I said when she hung up.

She shook her head. I followed her into the kitchen, which seemed to have twin microwaves, side by side. But she picked up something from the kitchen table and one of them flashed on.

"Dieter was my first husband," she said, watching the screen. "I was trapped under him for four days in a Lincoln Town Car. Every time I woke up I'd punch him. I kept thinking, what a sound sleeper. His skin looked burned and hard, and it peeled every time you touched it. When they told me he was dead I couldn't believe it. Now I can. Now I have no trouble believing Dieter's dead."

"You've got out from under," I said.

It was "Mr. Rogers' Neighbourhood".

"Where was this?" I asked.

"West Palm. We were young then. Dieter'd say, 'Try this,' and hand me a little black pill. I'd be out for two days. I think he had men over. I'd wake up so sore."

"Gosh. That's terrible."

"Yeah, it was definitely him or me." Still looking at the TV she said, "Old men. I found dentures once, in a cup."

There was a clumsy banging on the front door. We were watching Mr. Rogers take off his cardigan and hang it up. There was no sound, but you could tell he was singing.

When I opened the door it was the girl from the driveway.

"Do you live here?" I asked.

The girl had an empty glass in her hand. A bevelled tumbler. She just stood there, neither smiling nor unsmiling.

"Would you like to come in?" I said.

"Hazel!" the woman called. "Get in here this minute or I'll smack you!" She said it *smeck you.*

I stood back. So did Hazel. "This is not a mirror game," I said. I left the door open and returned to the kitchen.

"Maybe we should get going," I said. When the woman made no response, I added, "You are Lydia?"

She sighed. Her eyes went to the window. "Would you let me get dressed? And I better call Darlene. What's it like out?"

"Darlene?"

"Hazel's sitter," Lydia said over her shoulder. She was leaving to get dressed. From down the hall she told me again to fix myself a drink.

In the kitchen I hunted for it. I could hear Hazel making humming sounds on the front stoop and then came the boom and scatter of a tumbler on hollow concrete. When I reached her she was walking around in the glass leaving blood. I carried her down off the stoop. Lydia put her head out the upstairs window and shouted at Hazel that she had told her a thousand times not to play with that glass. I told Lydia to go on with getting ready, I would take care of Hazel.

I set Hazel down on the grass and for the next twenty minutes I picked glass out of the bottoms of her feet. They were slender sunburned feet, quite long. I got a pail of warm water—the water turned pink—and painted them with iodine and wrapped them in bandages from a downstairs bathroom. During this procedure Hazel hummed tunelessly. I found a broom and a dustpan and swept up while Hazel crouched to sight along the surface of the stoop and point out fragments I was missing. After that I got fresh water and flooded away the last of the glass and most of the blood. Finally there were only faint red footprints in a small circle of confusion.

I had found some Jack Daniels at the same time as I found the pail, under the kitchen sink. After cleaning up I sat in the breakfast nook and drank this with a little tap water and read the paper. When I looked up, Hazel was watching me from the bushes with her face against the window. When I looked up again she was watching me from around the kitchen doorjamb.

Lydia reappeared wearing a short blue dress and blue high heels. "My mother always dressed me and my sister like identical twins," she said. "My sister was a humpbacked dwarf." She glared at me. "I suppose you think that's a joke."

"It sounds like one but it's not."

She was looking down at the dress. "One day I'm going to have to find someone I can trust to tell me when to stop dressing like this." She straightened up. "Do you think men or women are sneakier?"

"That's a tough call," I said. "Are we going?"

"Darlene's not home."

Darlene, I remembered, was the sitter. "Look," I said. "We don't have to go."

"What are you talking about? I'm dressed. We're going."

Lydia noticed the pink footprints on the front step, and then she saw Hazel's bandaged feet and cried, "Oh my God, was it that bad?"

Hazel looked down to see. Her bandages resembled slippers and gave her the look of an improvised ballerina.

We drove over to Darlene's. It took some coaxing to get Hazel into the old Luxus, which seemed to strike terror into her heart, but once she was in she was fine.

Darlene's was just around the curve.

"Women don't have consciences like men," Lydia said as we pulled up. "It comes from not having power. When women get power they'll start having consciences. Not before."

"I never thought of it that way," I said.

"Maseratis and diamonds are nothing," Lydia said. "The only real luxury is a conscience."

Darlene's was a kind of house similar to Lydia's but on a bigger lot. There was no answer at the front door, so we went down the side to the back yard, where a woman on a chaise longue was suntanning topless. When she heard the click of the gate her head turned slowly like a blind person's. Her skin glowed copper.

"A man," she said, laying a forearm across her chest.

"Darl, are you stoned again and forgot?" Lydia cried, advancing across the yard with difficulty. Her heels kept sinking into the sod until she kicked them off. "Can't you hear the phone out here? Where's your remote?"

"Why?"

"This is—" Lydia was indicating me. "What's your name again?"

"Henry. What's yours?"

"Hi, Henry." Darlene had a handsome face, with a stately forehead and gold hair in a terrific mane. Her nose was turned up at the end, and it was situated too high among her other features. She wasn't a teenager but didn't seem to be a mother either. With a house in the westernmost suburbs, she had to be somebody's wife. But not necessarily.

"Hi," I said.

"You can stop looking at me now, Henry, because I'm practically naked here."

I redirected my gaze. Hazel was sidling towards a magpie. The magpie knew what was up. It eyed her as it high-stepped in a little arc.

"Okay, so what's the drill," Lydia said. Quickly she added, "Ah hell, why don't we just all go."

Darlene had risen from the chaise. She was about my height, a good seven inches taller than Lydia.

"Will Angie be there?" Lydia said. "Lydia to Henry. Will Angie be there?"

"Angie?"

"You don't know who Angie is."

I waited.

"But you do know Bruce," Lydia said.

"I do. My oldest friend." Bruce was Harris. Assuming this was the same Bruce.

"He never mentioned you."

"That's okay. When was this?"

Lydia looked at me, irritated.

"Do you know Bruce?" I asked her.

"A little."

"Isn't he just the greatest guy?"

Lydia's glance was the sort you might give to someone vomiting in the street. "Right," she said. "So we'll all go. If worse comes to worst Hazel can always sleep there."

I admit it had given me a tug to realize that Lydia, who lived in my own city, already seemed to know Bruce at least a little, whereas I hadn't seen him for twenty-five years. I turned to Darlene. "Do you know Bruce?"

Hazel was sitting on the grass with one leg in the air. Darlene was checking her foot like the prince with the slipper. She shot a glance at Lydia, who looked away. "Yeah, I know Bruce." She laughed and set down Hazel's foot.

"You both know Bruce," I said as I watched Darlene walk towards the house.

"Hardly at all." Lydia had stretched out on Darlene's chaise and closed her eyes.

"I too know Bruce," I said. "He saved me once."

"Nobody saves anybody," Lydia said.

———————

At the north end of the street beyond the pavement, where the washboard started to climb a little, just before the yellow checkerboard sign at the edge of a sixty-foot bluff down to the Falloon River, if you took the crushed-stone driveway on your right you wound through birch and poplars and after a short time you came to a white frame house with gables facing north over the river, and this was the Harrises'.

It was a big white house filled with light. It had three picture windows, in the living room, the sunroom, and the rec room. It was not a particularly magnificent house, just realer than real. In the sunroom overlooking the valley Mrs. Harris, an invalid, sat at a white grand and played Chopin or Liszt. Other times she plucked a nearby harp and sang. On my way upstairs to Harris's room I would strain over the banister for a glimpse of her in her powder-grey negligée. Once I burst up into the kitchen from the rec room and by accident surprised her in a state of partial undress, and so astonishing was her beauty that I was unable to turn back or shield my eyes, I just froze and drank it in. Most of my time at the Harrises' I spent in the rec room in the basement, where you could hear her playing through the ceiling, piano or harp. The Harris rec room was not, like ours, rank with dog hairs and flooding but oak-panelled, with over-sized checkerboard floor tiles and a picture window that faced out over the valley at the level of that flagstone patio and the fountain.

Harris's father was a six-foot-four specialist in childhood leukemia. Home from the hospital in the evening, he would pass, unspeaking, through the family and climb the main staircase to his room. Forty-five minutes later he would come down dressed in baggy rolled-cuff jeans and a plaid shirt, and for the rest of the evening he would talk baby talk. Dr. Harris was the first man I knew personally who dyed his hair.

After church the Harrises would eat their Sunday meal while I hung around on their patio and watched the goldfish and waited for Harris to come out and play. He would promise to be out by two-thirty at the latest and he never was. It was always something. The roast had gone into the oven late, or Dr. Harris had kept everybody with a story, or it had been Harris's turn to dry. Sometimes he didn't come out until almost four, and not once did he express frustration or resentment about this. On the other hand, how could he have a problem when the problem was mine?

But when Harris was twelve his mother died, of her illness, and five years later his father's heart burst. The whole life of that family went bang, like a book slammed shut. Harris and his sisters were scattered to relatives. The house was sold. A gate went up. I never saw Harris again, until yesterday.

As a kid Harris was scrawny and handsome. His eyes were milk green with thick lashes like white bristles. For years we were exactly the same height and weight, but he was stronger. My feelings about the Harrises were so overwhelming that I was always begging Harris to wrestle with me, and I would force him to keep on until he made me cry by sitting on my chest and pinning my biceps with his knees. As I wailed he would plead with me not to tell, because he was afraid of his mother, that fragile beauty, and as he pleaded, through my tears I would see the enormous wet patch of love on his shoulder. Twice Harris had to have his front teeth resplinted from biting so hard on his shirt while he wrestled with me.

Later, after his mother died, and before his father did the same, in the last years before he disappeared from my life, Harris grew a couple of inches taller than I did and a lot stronger. By that time he had real stature. By that time I had lost him. While I entered into endless stumbling, Harris passed straight out into the world as one who saw exactly what needed to be done.

———————

And here I was standing in Darlene's back yard looking down at Lydia on Darlene's chaise in her little blue dress with her high heels off and her legs crossed at the ankles and her eyes closed, and I was thinking how with some people it's like a different species. In an old nightmare I am lost in history and hauled up in front of Queen Elizabeth I, with the hambone frill. Such an alien, birdlike creature the Queen is. So imperious of gesture. So drawling, so rapid of speech. Harris dwelt in a different world, and I chose it, and his absence did not leave me, and twenty-five years later I was sleeping on the couch. My bedroom was roaches and socks. I was waking up to the exercise channel.

Lydia started talking without opening her eyes. "The thing about Dieter, my first husband, I understood everything about him except two or three things, and I knew that if I ever figured out those two or three things, then he wouldn't have any more power over me and I could walk away forever."

"What things?" I asked.

"For example. If Dieter was on the phone when I was in the room and he had to say something to me he'd say it in a completely artificial way."

"Dieter had an image of himself."

"And why was that?"

"It was better than the truth?"

"Dieter was human, you're telling me."

"Sure, I guess so."

Lydia made a little smile. "That's what you think."

I told Lydia I had been married once. "My wife was great, but I started turning into my father-in-law. Staring balefully at people. He had this tic, half his face. I picked it up. The exact same tic."

"Balefully," Lydia said, not opening her eyes.

"My father-in-law was in charge of the Rotary soft money," I said. "Most of it he was giving to two poor, single-parent families. And then it came out he was sleeping with both women."

"Rotary action," Lydia said.

"It made me a big believer in shame," I told her. "Shame's like a contamination. Now I can understand how easy it is to demoralize a whole people."

"Tell me about it."

I looked at Lydia. Hazel looked at her too but I expect for a different reason. After a bit she came over and tickled her mother's nose with a dandelion.

"Don't," Lydia said.

Eventually Darlene came out in shorts and a halter top, carrying a gym bag.

———————————

Harris was staying at the house he'd built for his wife Sam's parents, who had emigrated to the Prairies from England in the fifties and stayed, whereas Sam had gone straight back to the old country as soon as she got out of high school. Just now they were visiting her in Dominica. The house was an hour west of the city, south-facing, on a rise over the Blackfoot River. All around was golden yellow prairie, but the valley sank into it lush and green, and the river on its floor was a shining path. The house was split-level. It had a cathedral living room with big fans, floor-to-ceiling windows, bedrooms off a high gallery overlooking the living area. As soon as you walked in the front door the valley was right there through the two-storey window. It was a nice space.

Harris emerged from the kitchen to greet us and introduce Vicky, a young blonde in a knit dress who nodded briefly from a long sofa where she sat snapping the pages of *Western Living*. Vicky's attitude, while distracting, did not mar Harris's composure. Of course her problem at that point was strictly us. But Harris had a strong man's talent of making total strangers feel gratitude to be associated with him and each other in any capacity, and I was confident we would soon all grow excessive together. Moral authority in the order of Harris's has a way of shoving personal pettiness to one side.

To be honest, I liked Vicky, and despite the events that were to follow I continued to do so. I liked the way, as Darlene started unloading her gym bag of pharmaceuticals onto the coffee table, she came out swinging. "What are you people, drug addicts?" I liked her, but you couldn't get anywhere with her. I am always amazed when someone hates me on sight. I keep thinking they can't be serious, surely they can be kidded out of this, but of course they hate that even more. As a matter of fact, unless Vicky had been jolted by our arrival into uncharacteristic behaviour she was not my type at all. But I went off my type a long time ago.

"So this is how your sort live," Vicky said, recoiling as Darlene offered her a joint.

"Not enough lately," Lydia murmured, taking it instead.

Fanning smoke from her face, Vicky said, "How can you do this to your minds? What are you trying so hard to forget?"

"We're not sure any more," Darlene said. "Once we thought we had it, but . . . I don't know . . . it just . . ."

Harris was in the kitchen crushing ice in a blender. He shook his head to the joint. I carried it back to the living room, where the conversation had faltered. I went looking for Hazel. She was upstairs on the balcony off the master bedroom, leaning over the railing.

"You're okay here?" I said. "You won't fall?"

I looked where Hazel was looking, and suddenly I was back

leaning out the dormer window in the white house above the beautiful Falloon Valley, gazing down at the goldfish fountain in the middle of the patio where I had spent so many hours waiting for Harris to finish his Sunday dinner.

"Do you want to see some fish?" I asked Hazel. The patio and the fountain had to be a replica. I assumed fish.

As we passed through the living room looking for a down staircase, I noticed Vicky was now in the kitchen, talking to Harris's shoulder. Darlene and Lydia were smoking in the living room, where I had left them.

Darlene handed me a joint. I took a little, and then Hazel and I passed on our way.

"How are you doing, Angel?" Lydia called as we started down the stairs.

"She's fine," I said.

There were indeed goldfish in the fountain, and Hazel could not have been more pleased. Agreeing not to worry about the bandages, we sat with our feet in the fountain, and every once in a while a breeze would lift spray, and Hazel would squeal, or a fish would give her a real nip and she would let out a whoop.

Sitting there with Hazel I grew nostalgic and started to talk. I told Hazel how Dr. Harris would drop off Harris and me at a bridge six miles upstream, and we would float down the Falloon River on air mattresses, and the water would be brown like the Amazon, and the sun would crisp our backs, and the plastic of the mattresses would chafe our chins raw, and cows would follow us along the bank, curious. And there were water snakes and bloodsuckers, and in places there was barbed wire just under the surface that could puncture and sink our crafts in seconds. I told her we carried glue and patches. I told her how in Harris's and my time children were still emerging from the Falloon shivering into their towels with polio. And I told her how by late summer the river was a trickle in a bed of bleached rocks, but in the spring or after heavy rains it became a headlong surge, an angry brown sluice that rose to the full height of its banks, where every April it sloughed great dirty slabs of rotten ice like broken pieces of giant sidewalk, and one time when it was deep and fast and brown I was standing in the muck of the bank fishing, and I hooked into a sucker being swept along, a sucker so big it pulled me straight out of my rubber boots.

I asked Hazel if she could guess who jumped in and rescued me from drowning on that occasion.

Hazel could not.

"Bruce," I told her. "Bruce Harris. I'd die for that guy."

Next I told Hazel how when the Harrises went away on holiday I was the one they left in charge of the weather station in front of their house, a white louvred wooden box on white legs, and twice a day I would ride my bike up there and take barometer and hygrometer and temperature readings, and when it rained I measured the rainfall in a calibrated brass cylinder, and the information I entered in a logbook that was kept inside their front door. This was in August, when mostly it was hot and dry and cloudless, and I told Hazel about day after day of pale sky and white sun and extreme, dry heat. And I told her about the excitement of riding up there and edging through the front door of the big white house into the floor-wax-and-potpourri drapes-drawn coolness. And I confessed to her how I would pass through the house like a dreamer searching for I knew not what, weak with longing, moving ever restlessly and fearfully on.

When I stopped talking it was Sunday again and I was waiting for Harris to finish eating and come out and play.

I told Hazel about this too.

After a while I left Hazel and went inside to check on how things were going. Lydia was on the sofa with a margarita in her hand. Darlene was on her knees at the glass coffee table, arranging coke in eight lines with a razor.

"Where's my kid?" Lydia said.

I told her. "Where's Vicky?"

"Vicky left."

At that moment Harris let himself in the front door, and he had a seedy look, the kind more often seen on the faces of old men, whose brain chemicals are labouring harder now for less certainty.

What had happened was, he'd been showing Vicky around the house, and on the wall of a guest room downstairs was one of his paintings, done on a rig, of a giant orange sun setting into a tropical sea, a flash of green. When Vicky said she thought it showed talent, Harris, growing thoughtful, took it down from the wall and broke it over his knee.

"That should create plenty of distance," Lydia murmured.

"I don't care how young she is," Harris said. "She takes me as I am or she doesn't take me. She means what she says or she doesn't say."

Harris shook his head to the coke. So did Lydia.

A few minutes later I crossed to the window still sniffing to check on Hazel, who had remained fountainside, sucking her thumb. I rapped on the glass. When she looked up I waved. She peered at me, or perhaps only towards the noise, twisted around where she sat. Then she returned to the fish.

"She really likes those fish."

"Henry," Harris said. "What do you think about what I did?"

"I think what you did took a lot of guts, Bruce," I replied. "How do you feel about losing the painting?"

"Listen," Harris said. "The point is, no pretending. Pretending is weakness pure and simple. It creates barriers and limits vision."

"What's a painting compared to the soul of an artist?" I asked.

"Henry knows what my colours are," Harris said.

"Henry's a bright boy," Lydia said.

"Anyway," Harris added. "It's academic. Vicky didn't make the cut."

Later we ate the casserole Vicky had brought and failed to take with her when she left so suddenly. Lydia made a green salad to go with it. As we ate we argued about whether or not the fact Vicky forgot the casserole meant that in her heart she did not want to leave. Lydia thought so, Harris and I did not, and Darlene refused to entertain the question since we could never know. Harris added that of course she would want to come back, but that was not why she left the casserole. She just forgot it. I didn't see how anybody could argue with that. Hazel yawned and laid her head on the table.

"Time for bed, Cinderbox," Lydia said.

"Let me change those bandages," I offered.

By the time we got back, Harris and Darlene had moved away from the table to the living room. He was making her laugh.

"Why don't you just take everything off?" Harris said to Lydia, who had changed into his mother-in-law's gardening overalls in order to be more comfortable.

"What, and traipse around?" Lydia asked him.

"We could lower the lights," Darlene said, rummaging through her gym bag. Suddenly she sat back on her heels.

There was a silence.

"I just hope she sleeps," Lydia said.

Harris pushed himself up off the sofa. He stretched. "Anybody feel like a walk?"

It was nice out, windy and cool. Thin clouds were sliding fast across the stars. The prairie night had been roaring on in our absence with no trouble at all.

Harris wanted to show me an eighty-metre trench he'd dug for his father-in-law. In the bottom he'd laid six-inch PVC tubing to carry the overflow from the fountain to a pond at the front of the house. The pond had a raised margin of trucked-in beach sand raked over sheets of polythene. We sat on this for a while without saying anything. At first Harris threw handfuls of sand at a buckle of polythene. Then he lay back and looked up at the sky.

"Remember, Henry, we used to crush pennies on the tracks?"

"How could I forget those days, Bruce?"

"Remember the time the vibration of the train jiggled everybody's off except two of yours?"

"I do. I'm never that lucky."

"Remember I asked you if I could have one?"

Immediately I was sweating.

"I really thought you would give me one, Henry," Harris went on, "since it was only a cent, not even worth that any more, was it? And you had two, and twenty-four hours earlier I'd, you know, saved your life."

"Bruce," I said in a quiet voice. "I'm really sorry. Please tell me you beat me up and took it."

Harris was still gazing at the stars, his hands clasped behind his head. "Nope," he said lightly.

"You know I'd give you that penny today, don't you, Bruce? You understand that, right? You must, or I wouldn't be here?"

"I don't think it's a matter of understand, Henry."

"I'm different now, Bruce, I swear. Remember the kid who always wanted to be an architect? Well, he isn't an architect, is he? He works in a bookstore, and that's the best part. He was a shit to his wife. Gail'd say, Be generous with me, Henry, but Henry was just being himself. I'm dead-ended, Bruce. My bedroom is socks. Tell me you know all this and it doesn't matter."

"Your bedroom was always socks," Harris said. "The point is, my love is bigger than your unworthiness. It always was."

I was taking a moment to assimilate this hard truth when Harris climbed to his feet. "C'mon, Henry. Palace time."

When we got back to the house the women were on the balcony off the master bedroom, looking up at the night. Lydia was still in those overalls, but she was hugging herself with the cold. Darlene was wearing a terrycloth robe that must also have belonged to Harris's mother-in-law. It was too small for her.

When Harris and I stepped out there, Lydia said without turning, "We should go."

Ten minutes later we had gone as far as off the balcony into the bedroom. There I was grateful for the masterful way the force field of Harris's charisma gripped us and the melding began. You could practically feel the waves of love ricocheting off the Palace walls. This was it. This was the type and foretaste of the redemption of a life of stumbling and unknowing and shabby lack. Truly Harris was back. To save this poor soul once more, as effortlessly as another man might pluck an ungrateful pup from a surging flood-ditch.

Downstairs the doorbell rang. Lydia looked at Darlene.

"I'm practically still dressed," Harris said. He grabbed his shirt and went to answer it.

"He's practically still dressed and I'm cold," Darlene said. She got under the covers. Lydia and I were practically undressed but less so than Darlene. We crawled out to the baluster to see who it was: Vicky, with Harris following her towards the kitchen with gestures of importunity.

"Back for her casserole," Lydia said. She rolled onto her back and put an arm over her eyes. This was on broadloom.

I could hear water running. I asked Lydia whether it would be Harris or Vicky washing the dish.

"Vicky for sure," she said. "Something tells me Bruce likes them dumb."

"You're not dumb," I said.

Lydia took her arm away from her eyes and looked at me. It was like someone taking off their glasses. Her eyes looked vulnerable and old. "One, I'm here. Two, it wasn't me in the Town Car with Dieter, it was Hazel."

"I'm sorry," I said.

"Yeah, well. 'I'm sorry.' That's what I said. Hazel used to be fine, okay?" Lydia put her arm back over her eyes.

I didn't know what else to say. This was information too dire for the range of response available to the person I was so far able to be with Lydia. We lay in silence.

And then Harris and Vicky were in the kitchen for a very long time, too long to wash a casserole dish. And when they did come out it was so stealthily I almost missed them. Like a shadow or other darkly insubstantial thing, Harris led Vicky slinking along the wall to where they might slip into the little den off the living area.

"So where are they?" Lydia asked, rolling over.

I told her. Her head swung to regard me, and it was a wan look.

My account of the situation, that Harris would be comforting Vicky before he sent her packing, was met by a violent snore from the master bedroom behind us.

The head of Lydia seemed to sag between her shoulders, a weighted thing.

How could I console her? Was I any less disappointed by these events?

Darlene crawled out to join us. She was wearing the terrycloth robe again. "I snored so loud I woke myself up," she said. "What's happening?"

Lydia indicated the den without explanation.

Darlene looked at me.

"Bruce is saying goodbye to Vicky," I informed her.

"Really? Let's go see how."

Reluctantly I crept after Darlene and Lydia, down the stairs to the door of the little den. By the time I got there it was open slightly, and they each had an eye to the crack.

"I don't think this is a good idea," I whispered.

"Honesty, remember? No pretending?" Lydia whispered, not leaving the crack. "God, I hate her," she added.

"I didn't think Vicky was so bad," I whispered.

"Her breasts were okay, weren't they?" Darlene asked presently.

"Average," Lydia confirmed. "Real."

"Bet you five dollars she takes off her own dress," Darlene whispered.

Lydia came away from the crack and put her head close to mine. "Don't you just love her?"

"I do. She's great."

We both looked at Darlene, at least the back of her head, for she had not left the crack.

"I only wish we could see better," Darlene whispered.

Lydia glanced at me and rolled her eyes. "Video stores," she whispered. "A generation of porn heads."

"What'd I tell you?" Darlene whispered. "Off it comes. Gee, they're not bad. Hey Lyd, look at this."

Lydia did not look. To me she whispered, "One day it's reach out and touch somebody, the next it's the best sex is in the head. Social morality's an idiot in the mist."

"Somebody should take them a towel," Darlene whispered. "That's an okay rug."

When Lydia had stretched out on her back again, she said, "Sex has to be the stupidest thing there is. Rubbing and mouthing. It's too pathetic." With her fingers she flicked at tears that were running from the corner of her eye into the fine black burr of hair above her ear. When I leaned over and kissed there my mouth came away very wet.

She turned to me with her hand covering her eyes like a visor and whispered, smiling, "Darlene doesn't like you, you know."

I looked to Darlene. "Darlene," I whispered. "Lydia says you don't like me. Why is that?"

Darlene's eyes made contact with mine a fraction of a second before she returned one of them to the crack. "I don't much," she whispered. She tapped her watch. "I give them five minutes. I just know this kind of desperate sex."

"It's all desperate," Lydia whispered. "That's what makes it so depressing."

Time passed. I admit I was tempted to join Darlene at the crack, but somehow I couldn't. It wasn't the peeping, I'd spent my life peeping, it was the flight of all principle here suddenly.

"What on earth is taking them so long?" Lydia hauled herself up to look.

"It's the watched kettle thing," Darlene murmured.

"My head is really pounding," I whispered. "And I don't even know what's going on in there."

"Sure you do," Lydia whispered, not taking her eye from the crack. "My head always starts. I just hate this so much. It's exactly what hell is."

"It's tension," Darlene whispered. "Sex is a top spectator sport."

As Darlene said this, from the second bedroom upstairs came a tight-jawed wail of lamentation. If there were words they were unformed, prearticulate, their shapes cleft and blunted by the pressure of sleep.

"Hazel," Lydia whispered curtly. "She always picks up sex and suffering."

"Fifteen, fourteen—"

As Darlene counted down, the plaint from the bedroom upstairs grew gradually louder and more urgent. It was not animal and not human. It was not from this planet. It was a keen of supernatural distress with no earthly correlative. An aria of panic beaten elemental and smooth. And then Darlene had finished her countdown, and not long after, from the other side of the door we were huddled before, issued another order of cry altogether, from this world, a prolonged and fluting whimper, febrile and kittenish, and in the coy surrender of that, in its elaborate and spurious abjection, there sounded a familiar truth, of immediate import, and I knew that Harris was not the one I had imagined, and neither was he the one he now claimed to be, and I felt the force of him pass out of my heart, and the scales fall, and I looked about me and I saw where I was, and this was squatting apelike and largely naked on a sort of walkway down one side of the main-floor living area of a house under the prairie night sky, and at that same moment my two companions relaxed away from the door as one woman, released, for now, and so was I, and so also was Hazel, from whose room upstairs once more came the silence of a person sleeping softly alone, and I knew as in a vision that I must no longer dwell above the TV Repair, and I knew further that no longer would I wander the Harris house lost in my dreaming, no longer would I come to doors that I have never seen before, that open, when they open, into space and darkness, and my new rooms, above a 7-Eleven, are clean and orderly, and they have been rid of all things that crawl.

"So—" I took a deep breath and let it out. Leaned toward Lydia. "How do you find me?"

Her head revolved in my direction slowly, the eyes raging, and I thought of a crew-cut owl. "Do you honestly mean to tell me you will believe any answer that you are going to receive to that question?"

"Yes," I whispered. "Yes, I do. I will believe it completely."

"He says yes," Lydia whispered.

"I heard," Darlene replied.

Lydia regarded me a moment longer. Then she whispered, "I find you a lost soul." Although whispered, these words were spoken distinctly, as if they had been chosen carefully some time ago and checked since.

"I'm lost in you," I whispered.

Lydia looked at me, incredulous. The wonderful Darlene put her face in her hands and giggled.

"Don't encourage him," Lydia whispered to her friend. And then she sighed and gathered those gardening overalls against her nakedness, and with eyes no longer angry only tired she whispered, "Henry, take us home, okay?"

THE APPRAISAL

I STARTED a company, the computer end got into special applications, got a swelled head, got greedy, they broke away, we sued, they sued, the court ruled for them, Marketing said, It's been fun. A real learning experience, was how what was left of Development put it, and I was voted off both boards.

Fine, I needed the rest. I puttered around, got the greenhouse in operation, after all those years. Picked up some of that brown coin-wrap paper with the holes, for my bedside table change. Read a book. Read another. Always meant to read *King Lear*. Read *King Lear*.

It was great. Long walks. Life from a park bench, leg muscles twitching. So many mothers with kids. Solitary runners. Solo dogs in pursuit of their noses. Back to the house for a nap. Waking up in the morning refreshed. The reading.

And then one day, strolling home from the library, books in the knapsack, I passed two men in suits coming the other way.

One was carrying a toolbox, and I thought, They've changed the locks.

The bank does not actually want your house. The bank will do almost anything it can do to avoid possession of your house. What does a bank want with a house? It's the guys in the suits. You put a suit on a guy and suddenly he's a guy in a suit, and a guy in a suit wants his money. Or thinks he does. Thinks that's what a guy in a suit wants.

My key worked, but I had seen the writing. I picked up the receiver.

His wife answered. This was a Saturday afternoon. He was in the garden, she said. He took a long time to come to the phone. "Yes?"

"Mr. Pukinun?"

"Do you think my wife is likely to fetch the wrong man?"

"I need an appraisal."

"That's what I do."

We set the time, ten a.m. Monday.

———

It wasn't my house I wanted appraised, I wanted to keep my house, it was a cottage my wife and I bought in the days when she was merely bisexual. My wife is a high court judge now. Judges earn in the six figures with summers off, and so once after I showed up the wrong weekend and walked in on a leather-pyjama party, she offered to buy my half. Hence Mr. Pukinun. A name off her Rolodex, not mine.

I pictured an old guy, dogged. Heavy-set. Yellowing crew cut.

I was late. As it was, I'd had to leave the city before sunrise. We were to meet at the Shell snack bar in the nearest village, pop. 600, and on the phone he'd said he knew the place, the coffee was poor, and I was impressed. But I was half an hour late, and he was standing out front waiting, and he was not impressed.

He was a lean, tall man with sandy hair and steel-rimmed glasses. Anywhere between fifty and sixty-five, impossible to tell. Teetotallers without a weight problem hardly age at all. Good cotton shirt and chinos. White sneakers. A lightweight nylon jacket. Around his neck a first-class Nikon. He was standing beside a Volkswagen Rabbit with a diesel engine.

He got in. The cottage was six miles on gravel roads. It was easier this way.

I told him I was sorry I was late.

He told me he was sorry he was early. "That way I had to wait longer."

He asked me what I did.

I told him, Nothing. I read a lot.

"Reading is not nothing," he replied. "I'm a writer."

I looked over at him.

"I won a National Magazine Award for an article on the end of nature," he said. "A thousand dollars. I write about everything. I'll write about meeting you. I write five hundred words a day, rain or shine. My appraisals are pieces of writing. People pay me twelve hundred dollars to do full narrative accounts of their properties. I search records, I tell the whole story. My reports can be sixty pages thick. History. You learn a lot of it in such a line of work."

My foot was poised over the brake. "This is going to cost me twelve hundred dollars?"

"No, this one is peanuts. My staff is on holiday, so I fill in. Four hundred."

"History," I said, replacing my foot on the gas.

"I used to be a high school teacher. Social Studies. A pretty good one. Do you know why?"

"Because you like to learn?"

He looked at me quickly. Warily. "Exactly."

It was my ball. "Speaking of history. Now that I'm halfway through my life—"

"How can you know this?"

"I realize that the same again, forty years, won't seem any longer. Probably a lot shorter. It isn't much time at all really, a human life. But you put just five"—I took five fingers off the wheel and showed him—"five of these flash-in-the-pan little eighty-year spans end to end, and already you're back to Shakespeare. Twenty more and you're back to Christ."

"No, you must think in terms of generations. That is how knowledge is passed on."

"I disagree. Generation thinking is so we can tell ourselves we've been here for ages and we're really headed somewhere. I'm saying human history is a blink of the eye. I'm saying it's no wonder Shakespeare still makes sense. It's no wonder the Church staggers on."

"Myself, I'm a Christian," said Mr. Pukinun.

There was a brief silence.

"You won't find a piece of writing more immediate than *King Lear*," I said.

Mr. Pukinun did not reply.

I pointed to a log bungalow set back off the road, next to a beaver pond. "There's history for you," I said. "First resident on the road."

"Hardly," replied Mr. Pukinun. "I know him. Mike Boyko. A sad case. His wife and the beaver's mate died about the same time, ten years ago. Since then Mike and the beaver have grown close. Now the beaver is too old to work on the dam, so Mike helps him out, cutting trees, packing mud, and so forth. His big fear is the beaver will die before him."

"That's incredible."

"Not really," said Mr. Pukinun. Neutrally he added, "People cling."

A moment later he indicated the passing landscape. "I know this country pretty well. I prefer the Laurentians, myself. Vermont is also very beautiful. Even Muskoka."

I didn't say anything.

"I know your cottage too, now," he said. "Built in '53 or '4. Indoor plumbing. No electricity. Somewhat primitive."

"But very solid."

"It's still standing. As for worth—"

He seemed to fade into reflection.

Then he was looking away to the north. "On that height of land over there—have you climbed up?—there is a perfect circle of rock. Not man-made. And not from so-called outer space. A natural formation."

"Is that right?"

"Nature is filled with storms. In the atmosphere, under the sea, even in the earth itself. Such circles of rock are the result of convection currents in the very soil."

"Maybe they shouldn't all be called storms."

"But of course they should. It's simply a difference of velocity. And of medium. Should plants be called non-conscious because they move slowly? Just now I'm writing a book on ghosts. My theory is that certain states of human emotion are capable of triggering what I call storms in time."

"And there's your title: *Time Storms*."

He didn't reply.

A moment before I slowed for the turn into my driveway, he said, "Here we are."

It was a leaden day, and from the road the place looked like a shack at the bottom of a field. I knew it would be gloomy and dank inside and that Mr. Pukinun would not be impressed. I hoped my wife and her friends hadn't left dope lying around.

As soon as Mr. Pukinun got out, he rested his Nikon on the roof of my car and took a picture. While I was still feeling along the back doorsill for the key, he was walking down to the water to take another, of the dock. From inside the stale chill of the building, I could see the lake looking flat and metallic and depressing.

On his way back from the dock Mr. Pukinun stopped to take a front view. When he reached the steps he removed from the pocket of his jacket a tape measure so big it seemed to dwarf the building. He set about taking measurements.

"So are any of the properties you appraise haunted?" I asked from the screened porch.

"Approximately twenty percent," he said from around the corner.

"Sounds about right."

He came quickly up the stairs and through the porch into the main living area, taking everything in.

"People never tell me, of course, unless they're buying out a co-owner, but I always know. A certain fretfulness in the air."

"Are you feeling it here?"

"No, there's nothing here."

I admit I was disappointed.

"Do you have children?" he asked suddenly.

"No, no children. Why?"

He had picked up a cushion and was smelling it. "Someone's been smoking marijuana in this room."

"Can't explain that one," I said.

"The irony in terms of property values," he continued, replacing the cushion and poking his head into a bedroom, "ghosts are not a particular nuisance. Speak clearly and firmly. Explain to them that the solution to their pain is not here. Nine times out of ten they will pack up and leave within the hour. Just try that with a bat colony."

"Bats we don't have."

"Emotion," said Mr. Pukinun, "is the most rational form of energy in the physical world."

I nodded.

He sniffed the air. "Perhaps one or two."

"Bats?"

He nodded.

Then he raised his chin and pointed to the underside. I immediately thought *jugular*, he had a couple of holes he wanted me to see, but next he indicated what seemed to be his ear, and the roof of his mouth.

"These muscles," he said, "are homologous. Until recently physiologists could not understand why. Or what their physical purpose could possibly be. Now they know they are traces of gill structure. Phylogenetic memory. The presence of the past."

"There's a title for you," I said.

"What did you pay for this place?" he asked.

I told him, and the purchase date.

"I would say you paid a premium price," he replied, scanning the ceiling.

"So what do you think it's worth?"

He quoted a figure.

I was stunned. "But that's so low!"

I am sure he had come up against this moment many times. He faced me squarely. "Running water, I grant you. But no electricity. Propane gas for lights, refrigeration, cooking. The hundred-pound tanks, with no delivery. Wood stove. Minimal insulation. Limited access in winter, assuming you could live here in winter. A hundred and fifty foot frontage?"

I nodded.

He shrugged.

"Maybe last year you could get more. Now nothing is selling. The West has entered a long economic as well as moral decline. There will be fluctuations, of course, but overall the path for some time now has been inexorably downward, and it will continue to be so."

"Who says?"

"All analysts except the crank fringe. Driving up here you must have seen the outboards, sailboats, campers, snowmobiles, second cars, and so forth for sale on people's lawns."

I had.

"When you passed lakes you saw the vacation properties. The extras are the first to go, and they go cheaply. Very cheaply."

As we got back into the car he said, "Perhaps you should hold on to this place. Insulate it properly. You may have to live here before long. Difficult times are coming."

"How difficult?"

Mr. Pukinun smiled. "Blood on the moon. Stars falling from the sky. Sun black as sackcloth. And that is just the beginning."

"That does sound difficult," I said.

He turned his face to the passenger window. "These are metaphors, of course."

———————

On the drive back to town I said, "I used to be a Christian once. In 1961 I gave my heart to Christ at a Jim and Tammy Bakker puppet show in the Orange Hall. He's from Michigan, you know. She's from Minnesota. They started out small, criss-crossing the border."

"Those two were never not small," Mr. Pukinun said scornfully. "This is why you're not a Christian today. God is not a motorhome salesman."

"No, Jim and Tammy did their job. Why I'm not a Christian today is, a few years later I asked the minister of our church why the Old Testament God and the New Testament God have such different personalities."

"A very good question," said Mr. Pukinun. "How old were you then?"

"First he denied there was any difference. Then he wanted to know where I got the idea. I told him I'd been reading a book called *A History of the Jews*. 'My son,' he said, 'you've been reading the wrong books.'"

"There are no wrong books," said Mr. Pukinun fiercely. "The man was as ignorant a Christian as Jim Bakker. The Jews are a remarkable people. In business I love nothing more than to meet Jews. They always go deeper into the possibilities. They understand history. This gives them a context from which to question. In Europe when I was a young man I watched them being taken away. I will never get over that. And neither will the world."

"The Middle East," I said.

"The human brain," Mr. Pukinun declared, "is a product of evolution. Its greatest achievements have been in the realm of the physical sciences, and these have inspired a technology far beyond any kind of spiritual or moral understanding. History is physical, and it is all of a piece. One day it will be over, and then the past, the present, and the future will again be as one, that is, as nothing. Space-time is merely—" he flicked dismissively with his fingers— "a momentary flaw in the crystal."

"What crystal would that be?" I asked.

"A metaphorical one," he replied composedly. "My way of suggesting the primacy of a ground of Being beyond our physical understandings."

"And our tacky little properties and our hopes for their value."

He laughed. "Oh yes, our greed, and the palaces too."

I pulled up next to his car.

He looked at his watch. "I have exactly forty minutes to reach an appointment sixty-five kilometres away on winding roads. If I eat my lunch in the car, as I plan to do, I should just make it. So. We'll be in touch."

He offered his hand. I didn't take it.

"One question about your appraisal."

He paused with his fingers on the door handle. "Go ahead."

"How do you put a price on a piece of vacation property?"

Mr. Pukinun gave a faint shrug. "I just say it's worth what I'd pay for it. Of course as a professional I compare it to evaluations of similar properties—"

"Done by you."

His smile came quick and light. "Of course." He was getting out of the car.

"You who believe the world is coming to an end."

"Coming?" He laughed. "*Coming?* Open your eyes, my friend."

And there, on the pavement, in the space between his car and mine, he cupped one hand to his ear and with his eyes rolled back in their sockets he did the laziest, most joyous soft shoe that I have ever seen.

Then he ducked into his Rabbit and sped away.

THE DEATH
OF BRULÉ

WE LIVED on Ninth Avenue in those days, north of the tracks, close to the top of the poplar lane that descended to the gates of the cereal mills where my father worked. Our house was a slate-sided storey-and-a-half built for mill employees, one of five in a row. A willow grew out back, as high again as our roof. At night the trains came through, close to the mills. They started so far away they might have been a nerve twitching in my skull, they might have been pure imagination, they might have been an imagined memory. By the time they might have been an imagined memory they were lighting up the branches of the willow and gently shaking my bed.

In my parents' house it was mainly jokes and routines. My mother had a trick of repeating as a belch the last word spoken. "But it's true!" I'd cry, and my mother as she left the room would belch out a coarse dead *"True."* Her inventiveness with popular song lyrics was inexhaustible, and she was always taking up a word or phrase and repeating it in song. My father would say, "What's got into you?" and she would sing, "O, what has, got *in*, to you?" If you failed to hear or understand something she had said, my mother would perform an act of enunciation involving elaborate painstaking contortion of her entire face. Like lovers in love with happiness, our family communicated in a private code of old comedy and past jokes hardened to formula. When the occasion called for seriousness, we would all walk around with our top lips tucked up against our gums as if holding back grins. Such behaviour was ritualized and all but invariable, and in our house it created structures of refuge stronger than walls.

Because there were also the rages. There was what was safe but unreal, and then there was what was real but unsafe. My mother's rages were immediate and came from nowhere. My father's were slow and focused fury. I could not understand how two people I loved so much could hate each other. They seemed to be tapping a life beyond the one we made together, a secret life of rage without mercy. Sometimes I thought there would be a death. There was the violence and then there was my failure to anticipate or comprehend.

When directed at me, my mother's rage though unpredictable was unerring. Only in its excess was it wild. Its message—*Wake up, buster*—was clear and invariable. It was the blow from above that swept you from the rut of your folly. It was once again the terrible gratitude. To limit its frequency and power I became like one of those birds who push a button to avoid electric shock, but the button does not always work, and over time the creature elaborates a repertoire of behaviour to accompany the pushing of the button. Except mine was a repertoire of non-behaviour, the bevelled equanimity of the little gentleman. Tulip Paradis, the girl next door, saw through me right away and didn't care, and I loved her like a slave. Intelligent adults also saw through me, but the others turned away satisfied, even impressed, because I took an embezzler's care to be agreeable. My mother's rages did not stop being unpredictable, but I clung to innocence more dearly for that. I am talking about the innocence of the poker face, of the anonymous bystander, of the shining hour of a life without hope. I remember thinking at the time what a brilliant strategy this was.

Virtue as disavowal. The armour of invisibility. How could I have known that this was only the common custom in my country? And like everybody else I was now a cool bland child with a seething unconscious.

At the end of my fifth summer, my mother went back to work as a Comptometer operator. At the same time the kids I played with, including Tulip Paradis, started school, whereas I was a year younger and my birthday fell in February, and with no kindergartens or day cares in our town I had to wait. During the two years I waited, Ninth Avenue became my larger world, and what I found out there I could not have predicted any more than my mother's next rage.

That my strategy of innocence was not going to help me in the larger world of Ninth Avenue I could feel in my dismay at the broken sidewalk that ran along our side of the street, at the refuse that strewed the ditch between the sidewalk and the tar-over-gravel of the avenue itself. I could feel it in my fear of the hot brown grass in the field beyond our back yard, of the wreck and tangle of the ancient cemetery at one end of that field, of the scummy grey creek at the bottom of it. I could also feel it two doors to the south, where Evelyn Foe, aged thirteen, in the conviction that her parents were slipping her poison, had taken to her bed, willing, out of love, to go along. I could feel it next door to the Foes, where Morris Padford, after a period of uncertainty concerning whether or not he was destined to become Part-time Slot Machine Emperor of Ninth Avenue, had knelt and asked Heaven for a sign, and a loud yet gentle sound from a clear blue sky had assured him that he was. But Heaven was no more amenable to Morris's hopes than the world was to mine. Not long after, Morris knelt to request that his empire might extend even south of the border unto the peoples of Buffalo, and God replied, "Morris, you can't grow hair on an egg." And so the Padford basement gradually filled with unplaced slot machines until they stretched from wall to wall, and Tulip Paradis and I would crawl or walk on their flat, red, iron tops from the stairs to the furnace to the two dusty little windows and back again. We would travel on our knees to the centre of the basement and stretch out on our backs, suspended on a glut of slot machines, and even as I lay spread-eagled next to Tulip Paradis I would be afraid.

That my strategy would not help me in the larger world I also saw in the mad light in Albert Knight's eyes when he came to our door to borrow our sump pump for use in his back yard. Our neighbour directly to the south and, like Morris Padford, a colleague of my father's at the mills, Albert had erected a ten-foot fibreglass Niagara Falls left over from a trade show and wanted to pump water over it. Until his unprecedented appearance at our door, Albert Knight had been known to me principally as a feeder. Having trained his body to ignore all mealtimes, Albert ate only when he was starving, like a snake. In this he was unlike Morris Padford, who refused to eat anything for his evening meal except beef, potatoes, and carrots, and in case he had to be somewhere that these foods were not served, carried with him at all times a pocket flask of beef, potato, and carrot broth. But once Albert Knight had got Niagara Falls erected in his back yard—with a pond at the base of it containing our sump pump, to which was attached a hose that carried water up the back and so over the front of the Falls—he forgot his training and behaved instead exactly as if he had a swimming pool, lounging alongside it in a nylon-webbed aluminum chair, sunbathing and drinking large quantities of beer while the sun shone.

Watching Albert through the fence I knew that I did not understand. And my parents in the best of moods were not disposed to explain. My father's allusions to the world I found abstract and useless. My mother's were jokes and sarcasm that went straight to the point, or seemed to, but mysteriously. In my mother's version madness and evil were indistinguishable from stupidity and poor judgement and the quick slide into dirt and foulness. What an idiot Hitler had been to think he could pull something like that and get away with it. And yet victims too were fools, lacking sense. What the hell had they expected? Whoever told them the world was a kind place? Poverty was comparable if not similar folly, to be regarded with suspicion and dismay. Intractable as cars jacked up on blocks in dirt yards, as bingo line-ups, as rooms stinking of cat, stale coats, oil smoke, cabbage.

During the first of my two years alone I was in the care of a woman named Ida Ellerby, who lived on Ninth Avenue South. I hated Ida Ellerby because she refused to take my dog Pepper, who consequently had to spend the days tied up at home. I remember the scratchy pea-green couch in the darkness of the Ellerby front room and the mean cooked-cabbage gloom of that house, and I remember Ida Ellerby's beautiful red-haired daughter Elizabeth, who smelled sweetly cerealish, like the skin of my arm in the hot sun. In particular I remember one lunch hour, when Elizabeth went into her bedroom off the kitchen, behind the door, which she did not quite close, to change out of her skirt into her jeans, and I stepped up to the crevice between the jamb and the hinge edge of the door to see Elizabeth if I could without her skirt; I wanted to see her legs, and at that moment Ida Ellerby came back into the kitchen and with a curious satisfaction as of confirmation said quietly, "You dirty child."

I looked at her. What was this? I needed to know because in my heart I felt Ida Ellerby was right, and yet I could not understand what she was telling me, and I wondered if this was still another flaw in my strategy: when you know you are not who you pretend to be you are vulnerable to the craziest charges, if they are sincere.

The next year, my last before school, I had Pepper with me,

because I was put in the general care of our next-door neighbour to the north, Agathe Paradis, mother of Tulip, already in Grade Two. Agathe Paradis was a three-hundred-pound woman who was not French-Canadian like her husband, Jim, but truly French, from a village near Aix-en-Provence. She would stand by our front step and talk to my mother, and after a while she would say, "I got to go now and wash my hairs," and walk back over to her place. Agathe had met Jim in the war and loved North America. I once heard her tell my mother that the Mediterranean was not worth so much to her as the blue in her toilet bowl. As I write this, the chemical ice-and-flowers smell of that blue has come back to me, and so has the smell of cigarette smoke in the Paradis house, for Agathe was the mother of fourteen children, and everyone in that house over the age of fifteen smoked. Agathe was always in the kitchen, cooking and smoking, and along with the meat-and-beans smell of her food was the smell of her cigarettes. As a child I was a silent member of the Paradis family, lost in their loudness, among smoke and numbers, or behind the furniture with Tulip.

The Paradises had a sixty-year-old African Grey parrot named Brulé who always noticed me. "Hey kid," he would say. "What are you doing here?" Brulé on his perch was a household god, observing. Warm summer evenings he would sit out on the front lawn with Jim Paradis when Jim read the paper. Brulé had been present at Jim's arrival on this earth fifty-five years earlier, and the two were old friends. Brulé's observations were laced with French-Canadian jive talk from Jim's adolescence. Now white-haired, Jim Paradis had a long, loud yawn he often indulged on those warm evenings, as well as a remarkably violent sneeze with a tremendous shout component, and Brulé had both down perfectly. Brulé could also do the sound, from inside the house, of the Paradises' toilet flushing. He could do Agathe Paradis calling Tulip's sisters The Twins, who shared one mind between them and needed to be called again and again, especially since they could never be sure who was calling them. Another thing Brulé liked to do was insert loops into exchanges between Jim and Agathe. Agathe would say, "Jim, you get in here," and in the voice of Jim, Brulé would say, "What?" and in the voice of Agathe he would reply, "I told you get in here," and in the voice of Jim, Brulé would answer, "Okay, okay, okay," and Jim would still be absorbed in his paper and Agathe would still be inside the house waiting for him to come in.

Brulé broke all rules of what a parrot is supposed to be. It was clear to me as I spent hours alone with him that he was fully intelligent. TV had come in, and the Paradises owned the first set on Ninth Avenue; it was a seventeen-inch Philco. In order to have colour TV, Jim taped across the screen a sheet of clear plastic in three horizontal shades: blue at the top, green in the middle, brown at the bottom. Brulé loved TV, particularly action shows, which he would watch in an engrossed way and ever after reproduce all sound effects perfectly. He especially enjoyed Kate Smith. Lesser women as well, but only if their clothes were in disarray. When he found the action too slow, he would say, "Turn it off, kid. This is boring." In his later years Brulé preferred to spend summer evenings dozing outside on his perch, often alone. When he saw my dog Pepper, who in his presence assumed a sneaking or sheepish expression, he would say, "Get out of here, dog," or sometimes, "Kid, kick that dog," and Pepper would back away like a culprit. When Brulé saw a sparrow or a robin he would say, "Bird, get over here." When a Paradis cat skulked around his perch he would make the sounds of falling and exploding bombs he had learned from watching "You Are There." Brulé could do Walter Cronkite better than Walter Cronkite could.

I spent weeks that year trying to get Brulé to do the Woody Woodpecker laugh, wah-cah-cah-cah-cehh-ceh, but Brulé would go silent and turn away. Finally one day I said, "Okay Brulé, I give up," and as I walked away I heard Brulé mutter in a scathing voice, "Woody Woodpecker."

My dog Pepper was a handsome Dalmatian with a head and muzzle unusually broad for the breed. His manner was both noble and sly, like a fallen angel's. As Jesus's would be to me for a short period several years later, Pepper's attentiveness was gratifying, a source of comfort, although for the most part I assumed he was an adjunct of me and treated him with the same callousness I had been taught for myself. Pepper always wanted to come with me, but this was not always possible, or I would not feel like having him along, and I would shower him with shouts and slaps. Pepper chastised became a cowering remorseful creature completely unworthy of his nobler aspect. This behaviour made me furious, and as I beat him harder he would press himself right down into the ground, cringing into abject flatness while holding me with his eyes. Soon afterwards he would purposely transgress—sleep in the flower garden or stretch the screen of the screen door with scratching—either for revenge or to assure himself that I had been correct in my negative judgement. On these occasions, knowing that he had done wrong, he would try to forestall punishment by crinkling his muzzle and lifting his dewlaps in an ingratiating, tremulous smile that was very different from the straight-ahead, tail-whipping, sneezy one he had when he was happy to see me. Once, somewhere lower down on Ninth Avenue, he had been shot in the leg, and he was terrified by loud noises of all kinds: gunshots, backfires, planes breaking the sound barrier. Thunderstorms and fireworks displays, even distant ones, made him insane, and if he was tied up he would do whatever was necessary to get free, and then he would run. After a major thunderstorm or fireworks on the twenty-fourth of May, we could expect him to be gone for two or three days.

The reason Pepper had been shot was his weakness for chickens. Aside from shedding short white hairs everywhere, Pepper had this one vice, very serious for a dog, like biting, the kind that can cost him his life. The one time Pepper was caught bloody-faced from chicken slaughter, however, he was spared. Instead of allowing him to be shot, my father paid the man for the dead chickens and tied one of them around Pepper's neck, leaving it to rot there for two weeks. I do not remember any trouble involving Pepper and chickens for a while after that.

The year I was in the care of Agathe Paradis, Pepper and I would spend hours next door in our house while Tulip was at school. My mother's smell was Tabu, and that was the fragrance that rose from the lower three drawers of my parents' long blond bureau that were hers. The upper two drawers, my father's, had another smell, of mingled leather and camphor and tarnished metal. I would kneel before the bottom drawer containing my mother's underclothes and lift them in slippery armfuls to my face and neck. Alone in my parents' room I rummaged through their drawers, their closet, their bedside tables, searching for clues to the secret life of their rage. But what I found seemed for bodily or perhaps medical use only, and I could not see how such minor paraphernalia could ever be intended to address that terrible passion. And yet there was something in the mute and clinical ingloriousness of these things now permeated with the darkness of my fear that brought me back again and again to my parents' room. But nothing was resolved, nothing, only new fascinations, new mysteries, new observances elicited.

The evening meal, heated or poured straight from cans, boiled for hours, roasted to desiccation, was like the jokes, a necessary ritual. I was twenty before I learned that food may be a source of pleasure. Before that, eating, like smoking, was at best an act of communion. When fresh tar went down on Ninth Avenue, we pulled away at its edges and chewed it like gum. The tender interiors of field grass could be eaten, honey sucked out of clover, riverroot smoked like cigarettes. Waldo Mulema, a big kid, said there was a substance under your foreskin that would make you strong, but I did not seem to have one and was reluctant to grow strong on

Waldo's. There were also, of course, wild raspberries, blackberries, strawberries. In gardens all kinds of berries lay heavy for stealing, as did baby carrots, prickly cucumbers, watermelons. Crabapples grew wild and could be eaten when not fired at a friend. Back yards contained every sort of fruit tree: apple, pear, peach, cherry, plum. In a pan of butter over a fire on the river bank we cooked fingerlings of perch and chub. I was never an eater of nose excavations, but many were, flattening them first between their front teeth like BBs on the tracks. Nor did I suck my thumb. Tulip Paradis did, as long as I knew her, and hers was always gleaming fish-belly white, spatulate and stretched long, and as she sucked she would twist her finger in her hair, and so always carried at the back of her head a flyaway cowlick.

It was not just most members of the Paradis family who smoked, it was practically everybody else on Ninth Avenue, including my parents. Even T.J. Burke, who was eight, smoked, and was required to steal cigarettes from Milani's Groceteria to support his habit. Cigarette smoke then was as natural as anything else, as familiar as the air in my parents' house. I especially loved, having been put to bed at an adult party, being gathered up by my father from the depths of sleep and carried out through the smoke of the too-bright rooms in their raucous throaty chaos, to the peace of the cold car and the ride in dreaming anticipation of my own bed. I loved the smell of cigarette smoke in the car and later the tobacco and alcohol on my mother's breath as she tucked me in, the hard wild adult message of it, hard and wild like her and yet like her at such moments loving, perfume in my nostrils direct from my mother's brain.

———————

Tulip Paradis was the twelfth of Agathe's fourteen children, two years older than I was. She was a thin girl with fine thick black hair cut in harsh bangs. My earliest memory of her is from when I was five. She took me to a foot-bridge over the tracks. When the train came she pulled two fistfuls of orange tissue paper from her pockets, the kind of paper used to wrap oranges, and handed one to me. We stood there, Tulip and I, holding fistfuls of tissues out through the railing. As the smokestack of the great steam engine passed under us, we opened our fists, squealing, and the tissues erupted to dance and lunge and soar above the passing of the train.

On the other side of the Paradises' was a two-storey red brick house, the home of Uncle Garnet, who had a foggy indistinct voice, and I can remember nothing he ever said. To Tulip and me he seemed a hundred years old, but I think now he was probably only in his seventies. Uncle Garnet never asserted much, or much that was noteworthy, but he was always kind to Tulip and me. He would stand at his door and pass out candy. One thing that convinced us of Uncle Garnet's extreme old age at the same time as it embarrassed us for him was that not only was his fly invariably all the way down but he never wore undershorts. As Uncle Garnet stood at his door or worked in his garden, Tulip and I would cavort around him, lunging grotesquely to catch glimpses of the gigantic appendage dangling in the shadows of those old-man trousers. Aside from kindness this was the only message Uncle Garnet had for us. Later, Tulip and I would try to replicate this experience by taking turns climbing into a cardboard box with no pants on and making it tumble in such a way that the other could catch glimpses of our helpless nakedness in the cardboard gloom while Pepper danced and yelped with strange excitement.

Though I feel no particular gratitude to Uncle Garnet for the limits he placed on his pleasure, it was a good thing I never saw the inside of his house. For me as a child a strange house was the most potent kind of drug. Swamped with light and smell, I would practically be in a swoon. On Hallowe'en, standing in a Ninth Avenue doorway, the alien interior decor, the exhalation of food, pets, damp, smoke, urine, wax, was as much a force as the rushing heat, the glare of the front hall. The houses of Ninth Avenue were repositories of power, citadels of mystery with incompletely imagined interiors, like dreams there was not enough serotonin to complete. Nicky-Nicky-Nine-Doors was a trick on adults, but really it was causing those unimaginable spaces to open up to our eyes as we hid in the night.

A door Tulip and I always tried was the one belonging to Albert Knight, who erected Niagara Falls in his back yard, but even when Albert was not on his shift at the mills, his never opened. Albert Knight was a heavy man with matted red hair that he called his "hair hat" because although red it was easily thick enough to protect his scalp from the damaging effects of the solar rays. As long as anybody was able to remember, Albert had worked the night shift at the mills. Every window of his house was lined with aluminum foil, and for years he was rarely seen in daylight. But once he had erected Niagara Falls he would emerge into his back yard wearing his hair hat, boxer trunks, flip-flops, dark glasses with lime-green frames, and carrying a portable tape machine and a cooler filled with ice and beer. The aluminum chair he would need to go back for. He would drape a small white hotel hand towel over the tape machine and place a stencilled sign on top saying something like *The Top Forty Hits of Jan. Feb. Mar. 1950*, with the *e* in *Feb.* a St. Valentine's heart and the *a* in *Mar.* a St. Patrick's hat. And Albert would sit by his Niagara Falls drinking beer and listening to the hits of January, February, and March 1950 against a backdrop of trickling water and the drone of our sump pump. Tulip and I would stand and stare through the fence at his oiled breasts, which were hairless and swollen like a girl's, as he compulsively straightened his sunglasses, adjusted the hand towel on his tape machine, took formal long swigs of beer, pushed his sunglasses repeatedly up his nose, and checked and rechecked the contours of his hair hat. Every once in a while Albert would rise to his feet in order to lather himself thoroughly with suntan oil. Sometimes, quite unpredictably, he would rotate in his chair and salute us with his bottle held high, saying the only words that he ever addressed directly to us: *In all and for all* and *Ninety-nine*.

"In all and for all," Albert Knight would declare ecstatically, lifting his bottle in our direction, with a complex series of facial expressions. And then he would seem to consider for a moment before adding, with grave satisfaction, "Ninety-nine."

For a long time I believed *Ninety-nine* was Albert's way of referring to what Tulip and I did when we rolled each other in the cardboard boxes with Pepper wildly barking, and I would glance shyly at the side of Tulip's face as she went on staring at Albert. And then I noticed that Albert concluded everything he said with *Ninety-nine*. It was only his station identification.

People claimed that Albert Knight believed he had been kidnapped as a small child and taken to Mars, and ever since stumbling upon this information he had divided his energy between pretending not to know he was no longer on Earth and studying his captors closely for signs of imposture. It was said that he slept wrapped in aluminum foil to prevent them from bombarding his brain with microwaves designed to cause him to forget the true nature of his predicament. There was, however, never any more evidence for the truth of these assertions than Albert's waking behaviour, which had not, after all, prevented him from keeping his job at the mills for over twenty years, though my father used to say that this was probably less an achievement than a primary cause of Albert's problems. Tulip and I would have died to see the inside of Albert's rather shabby company house, but we never did see it, just as we never saw the true nature of the world that Albert carried under his hair hat.

These were the days of caves and forts and tents made out of blankets. At the bottom of Uncle Garnet's property was a shed that had once been a chicken coop. Now it smelled only distantly of chicken and contained Uncle Garnet's lawn mower and gardening tools and not much else. It was a place Tulip and I retired to as soon as she got home from school. When we heard Uncle Garnet coming, we would hide under the workbench, and he would not know we were there, or I should now say pretend he did not, for soon enough it would happen he had stepped into that privacy for self-inspection with a liver-spotted hand, palsied and irresolute but intent.

———————

On matters of sex and sexual conduct my mother in those days was oblique and severe, and I knew that like Ida Ellerby she would consider what I was up to with Tulip *dirty*, and as such it would be an occasion for rage. I was reminded of this by an encounter between my mother and Tulip's older sisters The Twins.

The Twins were interesting to me not because of what they had to say for themselves but because of their failure to display more than the usual physical evidence of being two people. The Twins were always together, usually touching: holding hands or standing with their arms around each other's neck. It was only their constant togetherness that rendered them distinguishable. On Ninth Avenue, The Twins, with their tight sweaters, their pleated skirts, their chapped knees, their saddleshoes, were out-of-time bobby-soxers. The Twins could have been pretty girls except for a certain slack-jawed quality combined with a refusal or disinclination to accommodate their world to the one in which other people lived. Having never hidden anything from each other, they were incapable of hiding anything from anyone else.

The day I have in mind The Twins, who were then twelve or thirteen, approached my mother, who was sitting on our front step smoking a cigarette. After standing holding hands for a few minutes looking at her as she looked back at them, they told her how much they were in love with their boyfriend and what a difficult time they were having deciding if they should go all the way.

My mother took a long drag on her cigarette, turned her face to one side to blow out the smoke, and told The Twins they were far too young to be thinking of such things. She told them they were children yet and ought to be ashamed of themselves.

After a pause The Twins cried in a single bewildered voice, "But we're in love!"

"You're too young," my mother said again. "How old are they?"

"Who?"

"Your boyfriends."

The Twins laughed, like twin chimes. "But there's only one!" they cried together. And in a flutey, rehearsed way Lulu added, "There could never be another boy like Mikey!"

Savagely my mother butted her cigarette. When she looked back up at The Twins she hissed, "You disgusting pair of filthy little sluts. Get out of my sight before I crack your miserable skulls."

A moment later The Twins came along the front of the house to where I was playing with my Dinky toys. Holding hands, they stood behind me, where my mother couldn't see them, looking down at me. I glanced around to see how shaken they were, but my mother's denouncement appeared to have left them entirely unfazed.

After a while Lulu asked me what I was doing.

"Nothing," I said, pretending to be engrossed.

"Doesn't exactly looking like nothing," Lola said, without conviction.

For a few minutes they didn't say anything, and then, speaking together, they told me they were considering going all the way.

"To where?" I asked.

The Twins gave me such a blank long look that I began to wonder if they even knew. But then a strange fit of giggling came over them, more like crowing than giggling. I told them to stop being stupid.

"He's the stupid one," Lola said.

"Are you," I said.

"He hasn't had any Experience," Lola said.

"Have too."

"You and what army," Lulu said. Her attention must have strayed.

"Are you," I said helplessly.

Despite The Twins and everything they stood for, I wanted to wear saddleshoes and used to argue about them with my mother, who insisted that saddleshoes were for girls, whereas I had the idea that only the red and white ones were for girls, and a boy could very well wear the black and white. Finally, when my father took me to the shoe store and the clerk agreed with my mother, I blushed, started to object, then broke down weeping. I had not known that desire would have the power to make me so foolish.

———————

One day it was just Tulip and I in Uncle Garnet's shed. She was standing on the workbench with her back to me, staring up into the darkness of the top shelf, when she said, "There's a cat here."

She called to it, but it didn't move. Climbing onto my shoulders, she reached out to it, and still it didn't move. She touched it and screamed. We almost fell, but she clung to the shelf until I had my balance again. Now she pulled the thing towards her, and hair came down from the shelf on top of me.

It was a cat, sitting regally upright, its tail and rear legs drawn in close to its body. When Tulip handed it to me, it pulled my hands upward it was so light. Light as the body of a bird. No hair, eyes gone, only mummied skin in perfect composure.

"It must of froze here," Tulip suggested.

The skin was hard, grey, stretched taut on the frame of bone. The cat seemed to be waiting, listening carefully. We turned it over in our hands. It was a cat and it was not a cat. A perfect effigy. Once we had caught a field mouse, and it died of fright in the palm of Tulip's hand. A living mouse, now dead, or so we believed, and we buried it. This was different, life majestic, perfect, fixed. Not for burial but for looking and touching in a time apart. And then we didn't know where to keep it, so we put it back up on its shelf, where it must already have been for so long.

The next day we came back to turn it over in our hands once again, and like a dream it was gone.

Tulip jumped down from the workbench. "Where *is* it?" she cried.

Fretfully she went to the door and came back to where I was on my hands and knees pretending to check under the bench. Tulip had already looked there, but I needed to enact my innocence, because I was so afraid that she would think I had taken it that I hardly knew if I had or not. "I already looked there," Tulip said with exasperation. Suddenly she crouched and put her skirt over my head. It was dark under there, and in the higher darkness was a sweetly musky edible aroma that was not like the alcohol and tobacco perfume of my mother's breath in the night but easily as wild and true, and I held on to Tulip's legs and did not let her move away.

After that I was a child in love. The wonderful scent of Tulip Paradis clung to my face and my fingers, and though I could not believe my mother was unable to smell her as soon as I entered the house, I never willingly washed after I had been with her. I remember the last summer before Grade One, the wasps and the heat, Tulip and I inside Uncle Garnet's shed, me on my knees on the rough boards, nosing up under Tulip's dress as she leaned back against the wall, sighing, her underpants stretched between her legs, her palms pressing the back of my head. For the succulence between Tulip's legs I was a burrowing creature, nosing and sniffing and striving upward, savouring, grateful, ashamed, and in anticipation of such moments I was almost able to believe that my strategies could be enough.

That was the summer I began to have a recurring dream.

There has been a thunderstorm. Now the sun is setting, and I am standing with my back to it. In the east the storm clouds as they move on are stacked and dimensional, dirty purple. Suddenly a point of diamond light that has been winking in their depths surges and swells and fractures into a vivid, stately group of beings like a regiment or choir. *Heavenly Host*, I whisper as a rainbow issues insensibly downward until, somewhere beyond the horizon, it touches Earth. Slowly, formal as angels, slowly and yet quickly, in frames, the host descends the rainbow. And then it is labouring across the fields toward me, but as it approaches I can see that either these have never been angels or else contact with the Earth has damaged their perfection, has in fact caused drastic corruption, because now that they are toiling toward me, they are swaggering and reckless, pushing aside the small and the lame and the helpless, kicking out at the weak. This is the worst thing, worse than the fact that these beings will soon engulf me: these are not the living dead, driven by bitterness and evil, these are eager, joyful creatures drenched in their own energy, and the only ones who will suffer are those who get in their way.

Tulip Paradis, I knew, did not wash her hands and face before she went to bed. I was stunned when I learned this, and I would lie in bed with my own face and hands freshly soaped and scrubbed and my hair smelling of the vinegar rinse my mother used to get the shampoo out, and I would imagine Tulip across the driveway in her own bed, unwashed and greasy-haired. How could anyone live that way? Me my mother had just stood on the toilet seat and scoured with impatient rough strokes. Sometimes when she called me to the bathroom I would have Tulip Paradis on my fingers and around my mouth and nose, and my heart would beat hard for fear my mother would seize my fingers and press them to her face for a kiss, but she never did, and in her innocence she would scrub Tulip Paradis off and tuck me in clean while across the driveway Tulip herself went to bed with a sticky film of the sweat and dirt of the day upon her.

That was the summer it turned out that all along Morris Padford's problem had been not so much overgodliness as a slow growth displacing his brain that caused him to say and do unusual things. The collapse of Morris's slot machine empire seemed only to fan his enthusiasm. His next project was bringing water south from Hudson Bay to the peoples of Canada and the American States by turning a string of abandoned silver mines into reservoirs to be linked by pipeline. "God and His old buddy Gravity will do the rest," Morris told me with a sweep of his fingers whose joyous flow was a taste of the glory of God's dispensation concerning His liquid creation. In order to round up the necessary investors, Morris had a multiple phone terminal installed in his basement, where he stacked slot machines two high in order to clear space for an office. One day he summoned his wife and children down there to wish them farewell. "I'd better let you go," he told them. "I've taken enough of your time." A month later, from his hospital bed, Morris spoke his last words: "I'm going to hang up now."

Tulip Paradis was probably never in her bed when I imagined her there, because she went to bed much later than I did, so late that I could not imagine such an hour. What I could imagine was Tulip not, like me, soaking her pillow with sweat on school nights for fear she would never fall asleep, but immediately, dreamlessly unconscious. There was nothing simple about Tulip Paradis, she was not like her sisters The Twins, but I never thought of her as a person who worried. She—not I—was the clean one, the child who had learned blitheness so young it was automatic to her and shut out everything else.

At school I was the little gentleman, obedient and industrious, skipping Grade Three, while Tulip failed Grade Six, and so by Seven when I hardly knew her any more we were in the same class, and it was a surprise and not a surprise the day she answered a question from Mr. McElroy about the circumstances of the death of Etienne Brulé by shrugging and saying, "How should I know, I wasn't there." The audacity of this made me catch my breath in fright and pride to have once been her friend, but from Mr. McElroy's instant fury I knew that like a lot of things about Tulip the response was not her own. And then Mr. McElroy paused for breath, and Tulip with a still more brazen insouciance added, "The only Brulé I ever knew died was a parrot," and this was her own, and I would have given anything for her to look at me then, but she didn't. And I knew that her own answer would not do, either.

By that time Tulip was going with older boys, sometimes two at a time, into the back field, and I was on my knees at my bedroom window watching as she waited for them in her back yard, sunbathing with the top of her bathing suit rolled down, sucking her thumb. And watching her I would remember the last time I ever tasted her, in Pepper's doghouse, at the end of the summer before I started school.

The doghouse was lined in felt impregnated with his short white and black hairs. It had a front door hung with curtains and a sort of mat on the floor. A deluxe model: white clapboard with a black tile roof. You could turn two wing nuts and lift off a wall. That August evening, Tulip and I squeezed inside. Pepper wanted to come in with us, but there was no room. He whined at the door so persistently that I kicked out at his face again and again until he went away. It was already quite late, and I seem to remember my mother calling even as we crawled in, but Tulip and I stayed where we were. It really was a hot night, and though it was now almost dark, we could hear Tulip's father Jim still doing his stentorian yawns on the Paradises' front lawn, and we could hear Brulé the parrot doing Jim, although which was which was impossible to say. The rarity of such heat so late in the evening seemed to create a special occasion, out of time, and so did having our own secret world in the midst of our own known world. After a time the Paradises' front door opened and closed, my mother gave up calling, vaguely I was aware of the drone of our sump pump trickling water over Albert Knight's Niagara Falls, and of Pepper after a squirrel, maybe even catching a squirrel, something he could sometimes do, and from inside the Paradises', Agathe shouting at The Twins, though of course all these sounds (including for that matter my mother calling) could have been Brulé, and then Pepper was back whining at the door, and suddenly one entire wall of the doghouse lifted off and moved outwards and away. I looked up from my olfactory feast between Tulip Paradis's legs, and there with the immediacy of God's was my mother's face.

We were yanked out, one in each fist. Tulip was given a push, hard, towards home. Her underpants hit the back of her head, caught on her cowlick a second, and dropped to the ground. Hardly stopping, she scooped them up and was gone. I was thrown down and beaten for a long time. After that I was jerked to my feet, to be dragged into the house for more methodical flogging by my father, and as I came up from the ground I caught a glimpse of Pepper, sitting at the door of his doghouse watching me with humiliated and frightened eyes.

That same night, just before dawn, I crept outside for the balm of his company. Though it was still hot, he was in his doghouse. When I said his name, he pushed his head through the curtains of his front door a moment, then ducked back inside. When he reappeared he had a rag in his mouth, and I could hear his tail thumping the inside walls of his doghouse. It wasn't a rag of course, it was too big for a rag, it was a feather duster, it was Brulé. Still half in and half out, Pepper swung his head to one side, dipped it, and opened his jaws. With a breathlike *whump* the body hit the ground. Pepper lifted his head, his chin tilted slightly upward, and cautiously, tremulously smiled. And then, like a supplicant, he came crawling forward, to lick my face, and when he had finished doing that, licking my face all over, he sat back on his haunches and smiled again, this time fully and without reservation, without any thought for himself, with his dewlaps pulled high and trembling and with his long teeth bared and his gums showing dark in the faint light, he smiled. Pepper smiled so hard he sneezed, and when he had finished sneezing he smiled again and he kept on smiling, and from behaviour so craven and pathetic it was clear to me that this was nothing but an animal.

A few weeks ago my mother called to tell me that Agathe Paradis had died. Lulu came by to pick her up for a doctor's appointment, but Agathe was not ready to go. The old woman was eighty-seven and had been living alone in that same house for twenty-five years. My mother (who moved to an apartment on the main street after the death of my father) was the only non-Paradis to be invited back to the house after the funeral. There she found herself in the company of three generations of Paradises. Of the twelve children who have survived, eleven were there with their children, all of the men and about half the women with spouses, and several of the children already had children of their own. My mother said there must have been fifty Paradises in that little house and another twenty-five on the front lawn. The whole property was blue with smoke.

Tulip was there, a single parent with two daughters, one, my mother said, as beautiful as a movie star. Tulip—who now calls herself Marg—has spent most of her working life as a waitress, my mother said, but lately she has gone back to school and got her high school diploma. Today in the mail my mother sent me some stories Tulip has written, as well as a photocopied article about one of them winning a prize. The stories are inspirational. Only one has to do with Ninth Avenue, a Christmas memory tale involving the Cholmedy girls across the street. The photocopied article has a picture of a heavy-set woman, ill at ease and grinning, receiving the award from the chairman of the district school board.

On the phone my mother admitted that she never thought highly of Tulip Paradis. But seeing her courage in going back to school and becoming a writer, she realizes now that she was wrong. As soon as Tulip sent her the material, my mother called long distance to thank her, and during their conversation she told Tulip how once as she was lifting me out of my crib I spoke a certain four-letter word, and when she asked me where I had learned it I told her, from Tulip Paradis. As my mother expected she would, Tulip found this funny. I imagine she found it funny the way people who are a little bit horrified by something will find it funny, because she denied ever teaching me to say that word. My mother teased her about it, Tulip denied it laughing, and together they celebrated the riddle of depravity in the world.

THE NAKED MAN

B Y THE TIME I was eighteen it was getting hard to live at home. Instead of moving out I bought a Studebaker. I loved the Studebaker, but it made no difference, so I left it with my parents and went to Australia. My parents had a double garage with so much junk in it there was hardly room for the family Chev. By stacking the junk higher up the walls I made room for a Studebaker too. This was fine with my parents, but I was uneasy for my car.

When I called home there was always some problem about it. Even just sitting in the garage. Of course, it made parking the Chev tighter, and I heard about that. A few times I hung up with the impression there had been some scraping. My father had talked me into leaving the keys for safety reasons. The first definite thing that happened was they lost the keys.

"Tell me again why you need them," I said to my father.

"Safety reasons," he replied.

Reluctantly I explained about the spare key under the front fender. He listened dubiously.

Another time I called he told me the Studebaker was leaking oil.

"It always did," I said. "It's not a leak. It's just a little drip."

"That car of yours is making a terrible mess out there," my mother said when she came on.

"So put a piece of carpeting under it," I said.

"*A what?*"

The next time I called they had got in a mechanic to see about the leak.

"He says you need a new clutch," my father told me. "He says you should have arranged to have it started at least every two weeks."

"What'd he say about the leak?"

"There's nothing he can do about the leak. The leak is the least of your worries. Do you realize what this car of yours is costing me?"

I told them to just leave the car alone.

After a while it stopped coming up. Sometimes this was how things would happen. Their lives had moved on. As a kind of joke I would say, "So how's my car?" and in a resigned voice my father would say, "Well, it's still there," or, "You realize your mother won't park in the garage any more, don't you."

When I got back from Australia it was six in the morning about a year later, and I had no money at all. But my parents lived twenty minutes from the airport, so I waited until seven and called home.

"Hello—" My father's voice was damaged and incredulous with sleep.

"Hi, Dad, it's Dennis."

There was a pause. "Dennis—?"

"Your son, Dennis."

"It's Dennis!" my mother cried in the background. She grabbed the phone. "Dennis, you sound so close! Where are you?"

An hour later the Chev pulled up at the Arrivals door with my father clinging to the wheel like a shipwreck victim. His hair fanned straight out at the side, and he was still breathing hard from sleep. I threw my bags in the back seat and got in beside him.

"So how was Australia?" he said. "Are they ahead of us or behind? It was dawn there too?"

"Australia was great. It's hard to know where to start—"

"Feed it out slowly, over time." And he told me how with the way interest rates were going it looked like we'd lose the house.

As we turned into the driveway I asked, "So how's the car?"

"It runs, doesn't it? It's not as if I could afford a new one."

My mother was at the foot of the driveway with her coat on, waiting impatiently for the Chev. She had an eight-thirty hair appointment and made us get out immediately.

We walked to the house. As soon as we were inside, my father called a cab. "Think I'll slide over to the track," he said, standing in the middle of the kitchen eating a bowl of cornflakes. "Now that I'm up."

As soon as he left I flopped down on the living-room chesterfield and passed out.

I woke up badly disoriented. I was on a different chesterfield, and for a long time I thought I was still in Australia, but I couldn't figure out which city. The only thing worse than waking up from sleeping too long at the wrong time is waking up in a different place from where you fell asleep.

It was my parents' main-floor guest room. When I tried to get up my body was completely without tonus. I fell back on the bed. "Hey Denny." It was my younger sister Sophie, passing the door. She shot me the six-gun salute.

"Sophie!" my mother called from the kitchen. "Why don't you give Dennis a tour of the house?"

"No time!" Sophie shouted from the bathroom. "Nothing ever changes!" She was washing her face.

I stepped out the French doors to the garage to take a look at my car. It was not there.

I checked the driveway and the other side of the house. From the darkness of the garage I watched Sophie's ride for work stop out front and pick her up. I waved, but she didn't see me. When I turned on the garage light I saw that I had tracked oil from the puddle where the Studebaker had been.

My mother was in the living room with her hair done, sitting next to a beautiful young woman I had never seen before. I said my name and we shook hands.

"You know Lori," my mother said.

"I never saw Lori before in my life."

"Get off it," my mother said.

Lori worked nearby with disturbed children.

"Lori's staying in the spare room downstairs," my mother explained.

"I didn't know there was a spare room downstairs," I said. There was only my room.

"Well, there isn't now," my mother said.

At that moment a naked man walked past the doorway down the hall between the main-floor bedrooms. A door closed.

"Excuse me," I said quietly, my heart going. "I think there's someone else in the house."

My mother was listing the people she had invited to a party we were having that night. She paused, looking at me. "*I* know," she said. "It can be kind of a Welcome Home Dennis party."

"What was it before?" I asked with a smile at Lori, who smiled back.

"A naked man just walked past that door," I said more loudly, pointing.

My mother was continuing with her list. "Susan and Ed, and Effie, and the Rauches (the Cy and Doris Rauches, that is), and Aunt B.J., and Wade of course, and the Chatterjees—"

"Who's Wade?" I asked.

"Lori's friend. And Dave Arkett, and Tony and his wife, and—"

I asked if there was a bed I could use.

"Of course there's a bed you can use," my mother said irritably.

"Why do you have to put an edge on everything?" There was Dave's old room upstairs, she said. And could I please clear my bags out of the front hall. She didn't want our guests tripping over them.

Dave's bed was a double. I turned back the covers and checked around until I came up with two shades of pubic hair. I dropped these down behind the headboard and brushed away absently at the sheet. I sat on the edge of the mattress and rubbed my shanks. After a while I went to take a shower, but there was somebody in there.

I returned to the living room in Dave's dressing gown. Lori and my mother looked at me expectantly.

"I was going to take a shower, but there's somebody in there," I said.

"I thought you told us you were going to bed," my mother said.

"Can't I shower first?"

"Not if somebody's in there."

"It's not Sophie," I said. "Sophie went to work."

"Nonsense."

"I think she did, Mrs. Weatherall," Lori put in softly. "I heard the door."

"Well, I'm sure I don't know who it could be in that case," my mother said with impatience, refusing to be held accountable for strangers in the house.

"By the way," I said. "I've been meaning to ask. Where's my car?"

"What car?"

"The one I left in the garage."

"There's no car in the garage."

"That's what I'm saying. What did you do with it?"

"Why are you asking me? I haven't been able to park in my own garage for a year. You'll have to talk to your father."

"Well, I guess the bathroom's free now," I said, but it wasn't.

Instead of returning to the living room, I went on to the kitchen where I made myself a toasted bacon and tomato sandwich. I ate this standing in the middle of the kitchen like my father, I noticed, and then I went to bed.

———

When I came downstairs again it was dark. Lori was sitting in the same place in the living room, only now she was alone, smoking a cigarette and wearing a sequined gown with a generous neckline.

"Hi," I said.

"Hi."

"I guess I should change."

"You don't have to."

"I look like a bum."

"You look very nice."

My father entered from the kitchen with a couple of bowls of chips and dip. To Lori he said, "If that dress had slits you could call it a strange sequins of vents."

To me he said, "Help out a little."

In the kitchen my mother was mixing nuts in a bowl. She gave my father and me a look that said, *They'll be here any minute.*

"Right," my father said and rubbed his hands together while glancing around in vague anticipation.

She shot us another look that said, *You don't think you're greeting our guests dressed like that, do you?*

My father looked down at himself with his hands at his sides, spread and turned outward in a gesture that said, *What's wrong with the way I'm dressed?*

My mother made no reply.

My father grew silent as if musing. Finally he rubbed his jaw and murmured, "Maybe I'll shave."

An hour later my father had a bar set up on a card table in a corner of the dining room, telling women who ordered their drinks on the rocks, "I only have ice for you," and describing their Bristol Creams as rhapsodies in goo.

When he noticed me watching him, my father told me to take over. "Wade's shirking his responsibilities on all fronts," he said from the corner of his mouth.

"Which one's Wade?"

"The shifty one."

As soon as I was behind the bar, people started talking to me. Most of them when they heard I was a Weatherall thought I was my younger brother Dave, at that time in Hawaii. A few thought I was my dead brother Joe.

From behind the bar I could see Lori sitting completely alone in her place on the chesterfield, drinking soda water. As I poured my mother her usual—Silent Sam, a cloud of Pepsi, no ice—I asked what was wrong with Lori.

"It's Wade," my mother said, scarcely moving her lips. "He's ignored the poor kid all night. She's completely heartbroken."

"Which one is he?"

"Downstairs. Playing table tennis with Gwen Dermott."

"Who's Gwen Dermott?"

"You tell me. She tagged along with the Freibergs."

When the men had been drinking long enough to approach Lori and engage her in conversation, she talked and smiled but always sooner or later looked sadly into the distance as she took a long drag on her cigarette, and the men moved soberly away. A few minutes later, during a crush at the bar, as Lou Destaffo stepped in beside me to pour his own drink, I caught a glimpse of sequins in the hall.

"Thanks for taking over, Lou."

I was knocking on the main-floor guest-room door.

"Come in?"

Lori's voice was high and soft with expectation. When she saw who it was, her head pitched back onto the coats. She must have been lying on fifty coats, her body slightly arched. When I approached, she moved over a little to make room. I imagined her rolling down between the bed and wall and becoming lodged there. I took off my shoes and sat alongside her with my heels dug into the edge of the bed.

"Look," I said. "I'm really sorry about Wade."

"No, I'm the one who should be sorry."

"You don't have to be sorry."

There was a muffled crash at the door, and my mother rushed in with a cup and saucer. I could see it dripping across the floor. "Coffee!" she cried. "It's all right!" The cup and saucer clattered down on the bedside table and my mother dashed from the room.

"You must like him a lot," I said.

The front door slammed, hard. The blow of it shook the house.

"He's all right."

Suddenly there came a violent hammering on the window behind us. I twisted around to see. Nothing. More hammering. A fist! A flash of wild face at the window, mad-eyed and snarling. It fell away. Reappeared. Fell away. Reappeared. Heathcliff on a trampoline. More hammering. For a better look, I turned off the bedside lamp. Immediately the frequency and violence of the hammering increased. At any moment a fist would smash through.

"You'd better turn the light back on," Lori said. "I think he's jealous."

As I switched on the lamp there was a knock at the door. It opened, and my father beckoned. When I went to the door he put an arm around my shoulder and walked me forcibly into the TV room and closed the door behind us.

"Where's my car?" I said.

"Listen, Dennis. We've got a kid out here who's pretty much in love." My father looked away. The cartilage in his jaw danced. "Don't spoil it."

I shrugged out of his arm and went back to Lori. I asked her why she put up with it.

"Up with what?"

My mother rushed in holding an ashtray way out in front of her. "Ow by iddoo ums?" she cried breathlessly to no one. Keeping her face averted as if Lori and I were physically making love, she snatched up the unused ashtray from the bedside table and banged the other down in its place. She rushed away. Like a spun plate the ashtray took a long time to settle. *Wrowr wrowr wrowr wrowr*—I was stopping it with my hand when the window hammering resumed. And then my mother was back for the cup and saucer. "All right?" she cried on her way out, spilling coffee again. Immediately then, both my parents were at the door.

"Dennis!"

"No! Go away!"

But already they were inside the room, with people from the party peering over their shoulders like idle villagers. I sprang forward and tried to push everybody out, but once I got them into the hall my mother slipped past me into the guest room and locked the door.

"You're on the bar," my father said. His lips were thin and he was holding my arm in a vice grip.

My mother of course would not let me back into the guest room.

"My shoes are in there," I said.

"Socks are fine," my father said.

I returned to the bar, where people were helping themselves.

I was carrying more mix up from the basement when my father drew me aside. "Better come with me. We've got a major crisis on our hands out here."

Wade had disappeared.

"You check the driveway," my father said.

The driveway was all cars. It was a cold night, and I was wearing my father's galoshes without shoes. I didn't know what I was looking for.

When I got back to the house my father came around the corner. "Is it there?" he asked.

"Is what there?"

"His car."

"How would I know his car?"

"He's using the Studebaker."

"Who said you could lend out my car?" I cried.

"Relax," my father said. "We couldn't all use the Chev." He was looking over his shoulder into the darkness. "The river!" he cried suddenly and headed off at a jog across the lawn.

"Dad! The river's frozen!"

He stopped and walked back with his hands in his blazer pockets. "Let's go inside," he said. "It's cold out here."

In the kitchen my mother was waiting by the oven for a tray of hors d'oeuvres.

"Where's Lori?" I asked her.

"Where's that big platter? I want you to help me serve."

"Did you leave Lori alone?"

"Here it is. Never you mind about Lori. Lori's just fine." She handed me the platter. "Here. Arrange them nicely."

I passed around the platter, and then I started to drink. Eventually I went to bed. Some time in the night I staggered naked to the bathroom to throw up. The party was over. I slumped on the edge of the bed with my head in my hands, wondering if I was going to throw up again. But I must have thought I was sleeping in my old room and taken a wrong turn from the bathroom. I heard a stir behind me. I was practically sitting on my mother.

"Wade—" my father said.

"George, it's not Wade," my mother whispered. "I think it's Dave, I mean—"

"Dave, go back to your room."

"Dennis?" my mother said.

When I came downstairs the next day Lori was at her usual place. She was wearing jeans and a pale blue cashmere sweater. A cigarette was going in the ashtray alongside her hand.

"Is Wade still asleep?" I asked.

Lori shook her head. "Thanks for being so nice last night. Wade can be such a pain."

"Is he around? I never got a chance to meet him."

"I know. I think you'd really like each other, too. He was hoping he'd see you this morning, but he got a call first thing about his car."

"The Studebaker?"

"That's right. He lent it to somebody he didn't know all that well."

"Somebody who drove it drunk and stoned with a suspended licence and no insurance and the car's a write-off?"

"I think he might have still had his licence," Lori said.

HOW HAPPY
THEY WERE

D URING Eric's first two months in London the only person to show the slightest interest in his existence was his
landlord, Tony Spark, who belonged to some kind of
Eastern order. Gratefully Eric tried his best to believe Tony's version of Tony, the worldly-wise instructor, the man's man, the enlightened seeker. The bragging, the bullying, the improbable
sentiments made this difficult. But it had been Eric's experience
that sometimes people to whom he took an immediate and vis-
ceral dislike became his friends, and in the desperation of loneli-
ness he wondered if this might also be the case with Tony.

Unfortunately the ground of their connection was the Ladbroke Grove flat that Eric was renting from Tony's company, TS
Investments. The flat, in Culpenny Close, at the end of the Portobello Road, beyond the market, had been turned by Tony into a
set of cheap cold spaces with glossy hospital-white walls. In the
bay window he had placed a kitchenette, which he had divided
from what he called the sitting room by a three-quarters partition
of frosted glass, while the sitting room he had divided from the
bed-sized bedroom by a stippled white partition in shellacked paperboard with the resonance of a tympanic membrane. Entering
the sitting room was exactly like entering a dentist's office, the

magazines on the Arborite coffee table, the black vinyl sofa. Eric would step around the partition expecting to climb up into the chair for the drill and instead he would sit on a chrome and vinyl stool at a narrow counter and eat Marmite on cold toast and drink hot sweet tea with his eyes raised to street level and all he could see of the old women who passed pulling grocery carts were their bony legs inside worsted stockings sagging over dustbin sneakers, and cradling his tea to warm his hands he would think, O England, model to thy inward greatness. And he would think, Only an angry, greedy man could create a living space like this.

Tony Spark may have been an unlikely candidate for a friend, but it was through him, though indirectly, that Eric would meet Felicia, and with her he would fall hopelessly in love. She would come and live with him in the cold white flat, and then he was lonely in a more complex way, and when he looked back on those early hopes of his "first English friend" in Tony he could only shake his head and smile and marvel at the fool he had been, and he would pine a little for those first, innocent months in a foreign land.

Eric fell in love with Felicia the moment he saw her. She was pushing through the swinging door from the kitchen of a cafe owned by TS Investments, in Westbourne Park. Tony had been telling Eric to eat there since the first day he arrived, but it was a half-hour walk and a measure of Eric's ambivalence about Tony that it took him two months to get around to it, and when he did go it was mainly to taste the crushed fishbone meal he had watched poor people buy from the market stalls on the Portobello Road. He didn't know, or couldn't remember, what this fishbone meal was called, but he had heard that it was served in some cafes, and when he had asked Tony if it was served in his, Tony, though he did not seem to know what Eric was talking about, had assured him that it was.

Felicia, whose silvery blond hair was cut short and whose body was tall and angular and extraordinarily beautiful, was waiting on tables in Tony's cafe, but she wasn't like the other waitresses at all. She certainly wasn't dressed like them. She wore a thin black cardigan over a white cotton shirt buttoned at the collar, and when she reached across to hand him a menu he saw that one sleeve of the cardigan had caught on the top edge of the shirt cuff while the other cuff was fully hidden. In a kind of amazement he watched his hand come off the table and touch the exposed cuff.

Slowly she drew back her arm, rotating it to examine the cuff as if she would find a mark there.

"It's out," he said.

"Of what?" She wasn't an Englishwoman. And not Canadian either. American, it would turn out. Connecticut.

There was pale down along her lower cheek. He had to will his hand not to reach up and touch there too. The hair on her head was light and fine, like filaments of flax.

"That's okay," he said quickly. "Only, the other isn't."

"Oh." She bowed her head and tugged at her sweater, glancing back at the same time towards the counter as if someone had called her. And then she made another false move, very slight but distinctly false, as if she meant Eric to think that she had just remembered something. She hurried away.

The cuffs, one caught, one invisible, should have told him. The slow weight, he would not be good with it. But he would be no better with the pretence that what he was going to ask her for next would just be going for coffee, that the rest of their lives was not spread out in front of him. For one thing, Eric did not approve of his qualms, which he considered to be his problem. For another he believed in love, which would find a way. For another, he could already not imagine his life without her. It was destiny, and the reason destiny felt so off-the-rack was that it was surrender. The lamb of ego to slaughter.

The menu was handwritten, in a feminine script, photocopied inside scuffed plastic. It appeared the bonemeal was called queg, and to Eric's amazement it was offered with practically every dish. This time England must really be in a recession.

When she came for his order he said, "I'll have the cod and chips and queg, please."

"Pardon?"

He repeated it, pointing to the menu.

Her smile was cautious. "That's not *Queg*. That's *2 veg*."

"The Q's written like a 2!" he pretended to complain.

"Uh huh," she said, pointing to the menu. "They do that here. You should see their *sevens*."

When she brought his cod and chips and 2 veg, on the side was a slice of Granny Smith. He looked up.

"Queg," she said.

Eric could only gaze at her then, thinking grateful general thoughts, and also how foolishness, like a cat, will go straight to the person who least wants it. After a while he opened his mouth, but he had mentally rehearsed what he wanted to ask her too many times, and there was no sound.

She was still waiting for him to say something when a customer behind her whined, "Me butter is all melted into me toast."

She turned.

"Me toast is all soggy."

"I'm so sorry," she told the man. "I keep forgetting. I don't live here and I'm not really a waitress."

When the man turned to watch her hips as she carried his toast to the kitchen, Eric felt afterwards he would not have had to be a very different person to put out those eyes with his fork.

Once she was back in the kitchen, Eric fought to be objective. How wonderful could a waitress be and still be just a wonderful waitress? If only there were someone here whose perceptions he could check his own against. But of course already she herself was the sole conceivable touchstone in his life.

And then the wrong waitress delivered his bill, and the next time his beloved came through the swinging door she was carrying a tray of glasses, because it was true, she wasn't really a waitress. When she saw him still there, watching her, she may have given a little start before she turned her back to shelve the glasses. And then she returned to the kitchen without looking at him. Many, many times in Eric's mind they met, kissed passionately, made love, married, grew old together and were buried in the same coffin. He had come for his queg mid-morning, and now it was lunchtime. The place was filling with office people, queuing for a seat, scandalized to see him with his bill and still occupying a table. It would be so easy just to leave, to hang around outside for her shift to be over. She would come out chatting with her girlfriends and see him and hesitate, and he would step towards her, and her girlfriends would walk on more slowly, casting sly glances. But he knew enough to know that it would be no easier outside later. More anticipation and he would be even more nervous, and the waiting for her would seem crazy and frighten her.

And so he willed it. In the middle of the lunch rush at the Westbourne Park cafe, Eric crossed to the counter and asked Gloria, Tony Spark's girlfriend, who worked at the cash, if he could please speak to the woman washing glasses in the kitchen. The quickness of Gloria's eyes belied a certain blurred or blowzy quality about her. Eric knew she recognized him from the Thursday evenings she spent with Tony in the otherwise uninhabited flat above his own, but she hardly gave him a glance before she turned to tell one of the waitresses to let Felicia know that somebody out here wanted to speak to her. *Felicia.* Eric waited, pressed so far into the coats he could not stand upright. When Felicia came out from the kitchen she could not see him at first. Geekily he waved. She came forward, it seemed to him, reluctantly.

"Yes?" she said.

"Thanks for coming out."

"I didn't know it would be you." Her hand went to her cheek. "That didn't sound right."

Quickly Eric said, "Will you have dinner with me? Tonight?"

"No, not tonight, no. I can't."

"Ever? Will you ever?"

His voice must have risen. Gloria shot them a glance. Felicia seemed to feel it through the back of her head, which she bowed.

"After work tomorrow?" Eric hated how the persistence made him sound so callow. "A coffee?"

"Coffee," she said. "Four o'clock. Outside."

"O'clock," Eric said, meaning *Outside*. "Thank you." And he turned and walked out into a vast space of flat greys and empty whites beyond a fizzy incandescent veil of joy, letdown, terror.

By four o'clock the next day Felicia had been fired for this very exchange. Tony did not like his waitresses dating customers.

"Only Tony," Felicia said, having a mineral water and a cigarette, not a coffee at all.

"I'll talk to him," Eric said. "He's my landlord. We're practically friends."

Felicia was shaking her head. "Gloria told him it was you. He says it's the principle. You were a customer, period."

"Look, I really am sorry about this." In the gigantism of his love Eric assumed he had destroyed Felicia's life. It frightened him to think that his love should be unable to defend her even from itself.

"Tony's all right," Felicia said. "He is a principled guy. He's just a little insecure." She smiled.

They walked to Eric's cold white flat of humiliating ratio, where they drank two pots of tea in the bay window kitchenette, talking. After a while Felicia went to the bathroom and came back asking what was going on upstairs.

It was Thursday evening.

"That'll be Tony and Gloria."

Eric went to the bathroom to check. Felicia followed. From upstairs came a sound Eric had heard from there before but never actually identified. Now he knew it was a leather strap. Now he heard a woman's soft cries.

"In the *bathroom*?" Felicia whispered, and her hand moved to her mouth in pretend shock, and the fluorescent tube over the sink was curved to a double smile in the spheres of her eyes as she lifted them to imagine the scene beyond the ceiling.

When Eric and Felicia made love that same night it was in their own way. A week later Felicia moved into the cold white flat. There she soon found each day to be little more than a spell of winter light in a long darkness, and getting out of bed was the equivalent of lifting her own weight again. It was as if she were ill.

"I'm not ill," Felicia said, annoyed that Eric should think she would not have considered this.

It was as if the problem were Eric. A student, six days a week he travelled on the Underground to the British Library, where he toiled and basked in British history.

Once his step had been light, the spring of seedtime in it. Now he was an old man of twenty-five, dragging his shoes along. And really it was little wonder that his anxiety each night as he turned left out of Ladbroke Grove Station and trudged through the phosphorus gloom of the Grove had been gathering through the long autumn and longer winter to form the conviction that life was getting ready to blow up in his face. Leaning his weight into the massive bedroom door, he would find the heavy imitation velvet curtains drawn against darkness, and even if his beloved were sound asleep and breathing gently, the weight in the room would be an extra gravity, and the air would be jammed with negativity and despair and require an auxiliary act of will to fetch it down into the lungs. Sometimes in the dimness Eric would hear a faint scratching, and slowly as his eyes adjusted, Felicia's form would emerge like something in a time-darkened painting, asleep and on its back, and the right arm would be vertical with the hand limp, and the tips of the nails of the left hand would be gently, methodically, stroking that arm from the shoulder to the wrist.

And sometimes Eric would back all the way out of the room and walk down the broad cold hallway with its floor of mock-marble gummed black in the cracks with a century of disinfectant, to the unlikely enormous bathroom, where the gas water heater over the dark blue metal bathtub would randomly explode twenty-five to thirty-three seconds after the hot water tap had been turned on, blasting the metal housing high into the air to pause a moment before it crashed down into the blue tub like satellite debris. And there in the enormous freezing bathroom, if it was Thursday, directly above him Eric would hear, like Jehovah and Jezebel, Tony Spark and his girlfriend Gloria, counting ritually together, Spark's voice manly and harsh, Gloria's breathy and muffled: "Seventeen." *Thwack.* "Eighteen." *Thwack.* "Nineteen." *Thwack.* And sometime later in the evening, after Spark had left, Gloria would draw a bath and fill the tub too full, and when she got into it the water from the overflow would drip off the ceiling of Eric and Felicia's bathroom into their own tub and down their drain.

But as often as not Eric would not back out of the bedroom, he would slip from his clothes, just inside the door, quickly because it was freezing, and slide under the covers into the margin of warmth the length of Felicia's long body, and there he would rest his head on his pillow and gaze at her sleeping profile, with or without the erected arm, and he would try to imagine what on earth was to become of their love.

Later, in the night, Eric would wake afraid. There would be a rushing scrim of dreaming, cement-hard, and then the wakefulness would smash through. He would lie there trembling in the darkness, Felicia softly beside him, and sometimes one of her arms would be erect and sometimes the other, and all his little daytime errors and follies and self-deceptions would be huddled around him, beggars in a downpour, and Eric would understand that he would be caught inside tomorrow exactly as he was caught inside today. In twenty-four hours he would be awake and trembling as he was trembling now.

"If it's me just say," Eric told Felicia one lightless day toward the end of November. "I love you. I can change."

She looked at him, surprised. "Why should I expect you to be anybody except yourself?"

But for his birthday she gave him a tin drum and he did not know why. Because he was all noise or because he was not ordering her out of bed?

One day in early December she asked him why he was not more angry with her.

"Why should I be angry?"

"Why should you be angry." She was sitting up in bed, the bedclothes around her, rocking a little. "Question. Over a year now in London. How many auditions have I gone to?" Felicia wanted to be an actress.

Eric shrugged. "Three or four. It doesn't matter."

"No? To who doesn't it matter? Do you think good actors are rare in London? Do you think there's no competition here?"

"Love, if you've only been to three or four auditions, maybe that's all you've felt ready to go to."

And Felicia directed upon him the gaze of the defeated. It was as if he had already done his worst.

"Just tell me what you want from me," Eric pleaded, whining a little. "Please. Just tell me." And it seemed to him that his love afforded him the energy to forgive her anything. Easily. Didn't hers?

But Felicia just smiled. "You know, it's funny. You're so obviously the one with all the denied anger, but I'm the one who can't get out of fucking bed."

"But I'm not angry, love," Eric said plaintively. "I'm not angry at all."

The other night Felicia had roused herself to go for cigarettes at the corner pub. A hopeful sign, although it took her an hour to get ready. But she came back whipped, saying that the pub keeper had refused to serve her. Now, there was something that made Eric angry. Boiling away, he practically ran to the pub, and as soon as he got there he pushed his way to the bar and demanded a pack of cigarettes. When the pub keeper just looked at him, Eric started to tremble. But in the din of closing time the pub keeper was simply watching Eric's lips to hear what kind of cigarettes, and with Eric failing to say anything more he was watching his eyes to see how serious a nutter he was.

"Don't have all night, mate," the pub keeper said.

Once Eric understood that he could buy cigarettes, he went blank on what brand Felicia smoked and said the first name he saw on the shelf. The pub keeper tossed the pack onto the bar and went back to skimming a pint. It was not until Eric was returning to the cold white flat and was approached by a heavily made-up young girl with the knees out of her nylons that he realized the pub keeper had assumed Felicia was a prostitute.

"Can't you see I've broken down?" she asked from the bedclothes when he got back. "How can you say you love me when you won't let me know this isn't good enough? Are we in this together or not?"

She looked at the cigarettes he held out to her. "You don't even know what brand I smoke."

And then November became December and December January, and a new year was upon them, and each day Felicia rose from bed a little later and a little later until one evening toward the end of January, Eric arrived home from the British Library and she had not risen at all.

And Eric placed his forearm across the doorjamb and his forehead against his forearm and he wept.

———

But what about Felicia? Would she really have broken down had she not wanted so badly to move on while just as badly wanting to believe that this time she had chosen the right man? Well, she hadn't, and yet she knew the problem was not so simple as another wrong choice disastrously clung to. The problem was that all her choices were wrong, and since this could not possibly be the case, the problem was that sooner or later every choice she made felt wrong. Beyond this, the problem was her fear that things would always be this way, and with this fear came panic and lack of breath, and she would find herself in a waste place with a cold trail and a headful of uncharitable convictions. Such as that men start late and never catch up; that men have inflexible imaginations; that men assume the initiative, do not earn it; that men who are vulnerable are also weak and scared; that men had no more clue to passion than she did. Convictions, Felicia believed, of a disappointed woman. A woman who did not want to know that it had stopped being probable the fault lay solely with all those men who had failed her. A woman who no longer had any sense of what to look for, or never had, because there was something about her, something unknown to her or forgotten, and until she remembered and understood and made ruthless changes she would be attracted only to men who were guaranteed to fail her.

Felicia had left Eric for some time before she was able to leave his bed. Left him not for another man (she would always be proud to say) but for herself, searching, searching, until one winter afternoon she jolted up out of sleep before the image of a little girl pushing open the door of her father's study, her father tucking something gross and tiresome into his trousers, behind him a woman the girl did not know, her hair in disarray, crouching on her knees to pat the carpet with fingers spread as if looking for hairpins. And slowly, one spike at a time, Felicia's will crystallized around a search for the central lost knowledge responsible for this larger problem she was having with her choice of a mate. In imperceptible stages, even as she slept, her desire grew organized, her energy collected itself, until by summer there was enough of it to drag herself from Eric's bed in the cold white flat to a rotted-out sector of the city like a combat zone. There, in a small room in a row of abandoned terrace houses taken over by a colony of New Age squatters, she was able to concentrate on her search.

Alone once more in the cold white flat, Eric wandered the streets of Ladbroke Grove lost. Since that first date with Felicia he had hardly ever seen Tony Spark, or even Gloria, only heard them upstairs, Thursday evenings. One Thursday night late, however, there was a knock on his door, and it was Gloria, in a bathrobe. She did not look well. Her eyes were hollow, the interior of her mouth seemed black, as with dried blood. Though she couldn't remember Felicia's name, she wanted to speak to her.

"Felicia moved out," Eric said.

"Listen to me, luv," Gloria replied. "I got the chapter. She didn't leave any—?"

In fact she had. She had left everything. Under the tub were opened boxes of tampons in assorted gauges. Eric piled them into Gloria's arms, saying, "I don't need them."

"No, you'd find them uncomfortable. Thanks, luv. You're sweet."

The weather grew hot. Fruit and vegetables from the weekend market stalls putrified in the gutters while in the musty food stores old women without cats shopped for cat food. Quegland, Eric thought. He clutched at Felicia's infrequent invitations to dinners with the New Age squatters, where holes big enough to walk through had been smashed in the adjoining walls of the squats to increase the sense of community and where the first priority was total honesty. Over meals of egg-fried rice and big bowls of cabbage vinaigrette with nuts and raisins all the conversation was candid.

"Right then. Who isn't cleaning the tub? This morning I pulled a pound of hair out of the bloody drain, hand over hand. It was fucking disgusting."

That sort of table talk.

Once Eric called on Felicia at the squat unannounced, and from behind the door she told him in an almost inaudible voice that she was not prepared to see him just now. All he could do was blubber against that sad surface. Another day he called on her too early, and the young woman who answered the door came back to say that Felicia was not in her bed. Shyly the young woman offered her own, but Eric, queasy from her news, declined. A few weeks later, quietly, over coffee, her old passivity stretched taut upon a delicate armature of righteousness, Felicia confessed that he had called on her during her very first visit to the bed of someone else, someone she had got to know by sitting up with him the night he vowed to remove his testicles with a razor.

"Doesn't sound very New Age," was all Eric could think of to say.

"What do you mean?" Felicia asked quickly.

And looking at this woman who had been the bride of his life, Eric was not the first lover to be struck dumb by a glimpse of the distance between his and his beloved's understanding of the worth of her being, a distance as unnegotiable as the distance between reverence and contempt, and all at once Eric saw how his unhappiness would continue to increase as long as he continued to visit the squat.

And so when Felicia's next invitation came he made an excuse, and when another did not come soon, he learned that he was still waiting for her to understand how much she needed him. Later that summer he flew home, where he learned something else: one year away, and already he felt he belonged in Canada no more than in England. He had never noticed before how slowly Canadians talked, drawled practically, or how when they took up a subject they went on and on about it as if there were jokes and mysteries in the most ordinary things. And so Eric flew back to London and lived another autumn and winter in the cold white flat, but most of his time he spent toiling and basking in history at the British Library.

And then it was spring again, and Eric was lying in a hot bath in the enormous freezing bathroom with the window open, when suddenly his right knee exploded bright red. Eric jerked forward. He looked up and saw the pool on the ceiling, heavy red.

Like a fool he was drying himself. He pulled on his pants. The first-floor door was like all the doors in the house, massive. He could never break it down. He knocked and called, nothing, was moving away to call the police when his fingers turned the handle. And then it was the dream of shock and the dream of a different flat but a similar flat.

The tub was full to the overflow with blood, blood and water. It wasn't a bathroom, it was a bedroom with a tub in it, shag carpeting. Leather straps bolted to the wall. From the door he thought the knees were inflated devices, bloodied white plastic,

stuck to the sides. The taps were not running. The hair made a red
Sargasso. He dragged her, she was very heavy, slippery, as if she had
soaped herself, dragged her onto the floor and tried to empty her
lungs, to fill them with his breath, to staunch her gaping wrists. It
was horrible, everything he tried to do was stupid, was out of all
order, was pointless. After he called an ambulance he saw what
Gloria had written in lipstick on the mirror:

WHAT AM I DIRT

A week later Tony rented the first-floor flat to a family with
two small thump machines. Eric's rent cheques still went to TS Investments, but Spark himself Eric did not see at all. Another year
passed, the last, surely, the Canadian government would pay for
Eric to toil and bask in British history. And then it was spring
again, then summer, and one day Eric gave Felicia a call, still hoping, he understood that. But she had moved, from the bombed-
out sector of the city like a combat zone to just down the street, to
Notting Hill Gate. To be closer?

Felicia sounded happy, happier than he had ever heard her,
happy to hear his voice. She invited him for breakfast a week the
following Thursday, at six a.m., and Eric remembered something
about Felicia the loss of her had caused him to forget, and that was
her taste for inconvenience. Eric remembered, and he knew he
was easily willing to be inconvenienced by her. And then when he
made a joke about the time, she told him she would have been up
for several hours already, and he also remembered the delicate armature of righteousness.

On the second Thursday, at six-ten a.m., Eric stood in front of an
ordinary-shabby white terrace house on a quiet street running
south off Holland Park. He had rung the bell, but no one was answering. The sun was up, and already there was a misty heat. Eric

rang the bell again, and again. He rechecked the address. He stood out on the street and stared up at the windows.

Finally, at six-thirty, Felicia answered the door dressed in a white robe, looking as if she had just got up. Despite the costume she seemed exactly the same. Like the first time he saw her at the Westbourne Park cafe, Eric could see how beautiful she was.

"I woke you," he said, and he remembered how, in the cold white flat, when the phone rang in the night she would spring up to answer it still asleep, and her voice would be squeaky and out of control, and she would talk nonsense straight from her dreams.

"No," Felicia said. "I was meditating. Would you like some breakfast?"

"I would," Eric said. "Thank you."

Felicia told him he could sit at the table, and then she disappeared. It was a low table with cushions instead of chairs, in an alcove hard to the right of the front door. Eric was still trying to find a comfortable position when the door opened, and a voice he knew called out, "I'm back, where's breakfast?" and from behind the door one running shoe and a second running shoe flew past and down the hall.

"All right then?" the man said over his shoulder to Eric as he loped after his shoes. He disappeared from sight.

There was a grunt and the sound of effort, and then, "It's Eric, right? My Culpenny tenant?"

Eric leaned out into the hallway to look at the man he had once imagined could be his friend. "Yes."

Tony Spark was hanging in gravity boots from the door frame. His face was red, his sweatshirt had bunched at the armpits, and the black hair of his belly was exposed. His hands were folded across his chest. "You do this?"

"Never."

"It's a good thing to do."

"It looks like a good thing to do."

"Tell me why."

"Gets the circulation going? Gives the heart a rest?"

"The *heart*? Are you kidding me? The heart works harder. It's about circulation. Ten minutes."

"Twice a day?"

"I'll do it four or five. If I find the time, which is not easy. You're still a student? You writing anything yet?"

"Just the thesis."

"That's writing, isn't it? You don't dictate the fucking thing. Listen, I can give you Biros. Ten years' worth of Biros."

Eric had lived in England long enough to know that Biros were ballpoint pens.

"To me," Spark said, "ten years' worth of Biros—good Biros—is nothing. To you it's ten years' worth of Biros. Am I right?"

They had been married three months. Felicia was pregnant, not quite showing. Spark came down from the door frame, and they sat together across the breakfast table to tell Eric the story. In the days when she was still living at the squat, every Sunday and Thursday it would be her turn to cook, and she would shop at a health food store owned by the same modified Eastern order that Tony belonged to.

"For years I've belonged," Tony said. "I like to hedge my bets."

"I remembered Tony had some connection," Felicia said. "But I didn't see him again until—well, I'm coming to that."

At the health food store Felicia was soon picking up the pamphlets provided at the checkout and finding that she could relate to their spiritual message. The squat had never been a particularly organized or enlightened place. In this it was unlike the order, which dressed its members in white robes; put them to work selling Biros, flowers, health food; did not allow them to sleep more than five hours a night, the other three being devoted to prayers and meditation. Her name was now Piara Kapoor. One day she was taken to meet the Spiritual Leader, Bhai Singh, formerly an employee of Air India, and the first thing he had asked her was, was she married.

"No," she had said and flushed and bowed her head.

"Very good. I have exactly the man for you."

"The coincidence," Felicia said, "was just too incredible."

At that point Tony was not a full-fledged member of the order because he could not see himself managing TS Investments dressed in funny clothes, but he was giving them one-third of his profits. "I must have been crazy," he said and shook his head. Bhai Singh instructed him to marry this woman.

Spark shrugged. "It wasn't an easy commandment for me. Ranjit Sambhi—that's me—was a happy man. I had other fish to fry." He looked at Eric, and Eric had no idea what the look meant. Spark indicated Felicia. "She's not anybody I'd have picked on my own. She wasn't even a virgin, for Christ sake. But what can you do? It's God's will."

"The beautiful thing," Felicia reflected a little later in the breakfast, "I didn't choose Ranjit. I mean, I don't have to blame myself."

"She hates me for other reasons," Spark said and winked.

Felicia glanced at Spark with a small proprietary smile. To Eric she said, "Three times a year the women go on their own retreat, to Wales. It's a chance to get away."

"We're only allowed to rubber once a month," Spark offered. "But then it's in style."

"After four weeks you really appreciate it," Felicia added. She bowed her head and blushed.

"Enh, it's okay." Spark waggled his hand. "*Etsi k'etsi*, if you know what I mean."

While Spark was changing his clothes for work, Felicia sat on with Eric at the table. By this time Eric didn't know what to say.

"Bhai Singh has taught me so much," Felicia said after a silence.

"About yourself?" Eric tried.

Felicia leaned forward, counselling. "Eric, the past only exists as a problem."

Eric shifted on his pillow. "It'll always be a problem for somebody, I suppose. That's why there's always something to learn."

"Eric, if it's not a problem there's no learning. There's nothing to be done."

"Sometimes problems get forgotten."

"Is a forgotten problem really a problem?"

"I don't think I'll be joining the order," Eric said.

"No," Felicia said gently. "You're too attached to the past."

———

After breakfast Eric said goodbye to Felicia, who was leaving to serve Bhai Singh at his head office in Shepherd's Bush, clerical work.

"The majesty and bounty of God be with you," she said, squeezing his hand.

"Thanks for breakfast," Eric replied.

Spark was taking Eric to see where he was now employed two days a week by the order. "It works out a hell of a lot cheaper than a third of my income," he explained. "Now that I'm a married man, a kid in the oven. The truth is, they need me. You know how much they need me? I don't have to wear the robes. Do you realize how rare that is?"

Spark was dressed in slacks and a silk windbreaker. He was driving a newer Jaguar than the one he used to park in Culpenny Close on Thursday nights. There seemed to be something he wanted to say, and Eric was tensed for it.

It came at a stoplight. Spark reached over and gripped the back of Eric's neck. "So I got your woman," he said, watching the light.

Eric could not easily turn his head, so he watched it too. "That's right, you did."

"How does that make you feel, then?"

Eric was by no means sure yet, but he knew what he was ready to say. "Sad."

Spark took his hand away from Eric's neck ready to shift into first. Eric looked at Spark's hand on the gearshift. It was a seedbed for hair.

"You shouldn't be," Spark said. "She's better off. She needs a man."

Eric glanced away and then he looked at Spark. "How about Gloria? What did she need?"

"Gloria?" Spark was pulling away from the light. "Even you should know the answer to that one."

Eric thought for a moment. "Actually, I don't."

Spark was unconvinced. "What the hell do you think? Take a wild guess."

"I don't know."

"Right. Here's a hint. She was just as big a pain in the arse as anybody else."

"God?" Eric said.

"Give the lad a prize."

On the way to Spark's office they stopped at some kind of shipping depot on the Finchley Road, so Spark could give Eric an indication of the volume of the business, but there was nothing there to be picked up.

"Somebody must have got here first," Spark said, disappointed.

A few minutes later, pulling down the lane behind where he worked, Spark told Eric, "Remember, the name's Ranjit. I don't want to hear any *Tony*s in there."

As a result of stopping, Spark arrived ten minutes late for work, and it turned out that he had a boss, a hawk-faced young American in a white robe who wanted to know why he was late. When Spark admitted he had stopped at the depot, the young man flew into a rage. Embarrassed, Eric stepped outside and waited on the front steps of the office, where he could hear the tirade through the door. For five minutes by Eric's watch, Spark's boss railed at him on the subject of wasteful duplication of effort. It was the most brutal and humiliating act of sustained verbal abuse Eric had ever experienced.

"... and unless it's on direct orders from me, I don't want to see or hear of you stopping there ever again, is that absolutely clear?"

Fifteen seconds later Spark came out onto the steps.

"Gopal doesn't like it when I check the depot," he explained. "Here. Let me show you." And he led Eric down a corridor to a fluorescent room containing eighteen exhausted-looking East Indian women, each at a phone, selling Biros.

"We sell all over Europe, especially Eastern Europe," Spark said. "Shops, schools, boards, governments, prisons, every level, everywhere. The biggest operation of its kind. Here. What did I tell you? You're not the only pen-pusher around here. Have some Biros." And from a bin he scooped a handful of ballpoint pens and pushed it at Eric. He dropped his voice. "Just don't let Asshole see them."

After the tour, Spark wanted Eric to wait for him so they could go for lunch, but Eric told him he had another appointment and he hoped he and Felicia would be very happy together.

Spark seemed startled at the idea. "What's your point? Why shouldn't we be?"

"Thanks for breakfast," Eric said. "And for the Biros."

Spark walked Eric to the door. On the front step he looked at him closely for a moment, as if for the first time. He came closer, confidential. "Here's some free advice. Never ask a woman what she wants because she never fucking knows. Figure it out for yourself and give it to her in spades. You understand what I'm saying?"

"I think so," Eric said.

"Believe me, on this plane it works. And I'll tell you something else. It works for more than women."

"I believe you," Eric said. "But only on this plane."

"I said that. Didn't I say that?" Spark dropped his voice. "Get the fuck out of here." He said it almost affectionately. And when Eric looked back, Spark, who was still on the step, waved.

———————

Back in the cold white flat of humiliating ratio, Eric emptied his pockets of Biros. Altogether there were fourteen. Ten worked. He held the ten good ones in his hand a moment, hefted them, and then he threw them all out.

Later he turned the hot water tap on full, and when the metal housing blew he caught it, for the first time ever. In one fluid movement he snatched it out of the air and replaced it over the bank of blue flame. Then he drew himself a long bath that filled the enormous freezing bathroom with steam.

Later on, following a lunch of toast and Marmite and hot sweet tea and a Granny Smith apple in the bay window kitchenette, Eric rode the Underground to the British Library where he toiled and basked in history until the closing bell sounded at twenty to nine. And as Eric played he knew exactly how happy he was, and that was pretty happy. Sad too, but happy. Pretty happy, anyway. Happy enough.

WALKING
ON THE MOON

S UNDAY, and Martin had to go up onto the roof again. At least we don't have skunks, he reflected. Mammals are smarter than water.

Martin's daughter, Janey, who was thirteen, was still in the bathroom.

"The goons are up early," she said through the door, meaning their neighbours to the north. "Hey Dad."

"Did the goons go to bed is the question. What?"

The newspaper, emerging from under the door. Martin squatted in the hall to squint at it.

BUTT TAX HIKE EYED, he read.

"Oh, I get it—"

"I'm going to be a journalist," Janey said.

"First you're going to have to come out of there. I'll meet you downstairs."

Martin's son, Ben, was in the kitchen feeding his slime mould. The stuff flows in one mass through soil and rotting leaves, over and around all obstacles. Ben kept his in a Mason jar. He was dropping in oat flakes.

"A perfect day for the roof," Martin said.

"What's it going to do, Dad?"

Ben was not quite five.

"Raise me up. What do you feel like for breakfast, Ben?"

"What have you got?"

The toilet flushed. Janey started down the stairs.

"Wash your hands!" Martin shouted.

Janey returned to the bathroom.

"Froot Loops, bagel, oatmeal, nice soft bread, scrambled egg, peanut butter, jam, that's it."

The dog crept in, looking shame-faced.

"You," Martin said.

The dog went down carefully onto its elbows and nestled its singed torso into the crook of its big disc thighs, its muzzle low down and parallel to the floor, eyes upraised.

"Answer," Martin said. "I'm waiting here."

"Umm—"

Janey came into the kitchen.

"And you, Dog," she said and squatted to scratch its ears. "You don't have to worry. It'll grow back. Pelt-o-genesis."

"Stop being nice to him, after last night," Martin said.

"Aw, Pooch feels terrible about being insane."

"Grambled egg," Ben said.

"Achingly beautiful out there," Martin muttered, glancing towards the window, which was wide and high and in fact showed only the wall of the house next door, the goons' house.

"What we need is a visitor," Janey said.

"Not wet," Ben said.

"I never do your eggs wet," Martin replied.

"She does," Ben said.

Janey jumped up. "How can you say that!"

The dog's tail walloped the floor.

"We had a visitor last night," Martin reminded Janey.

"Pepé Le Pew."

Martin looked at her. "Pepé Le Pew is a guy."

"A guy *skunk*," Janey said. "Anyway she was your visitor. You're the lonely hunter. I was conversation fodder. Let's see which of us is more alive to this teen disaster."

"That's enough."

"She pass?"

"Yeah, on out the door."

"Roof," Ben said.

"*She*," Martin added, "had a name."

"Gwen. I know. For Gwyneth. You introduced us, remember? Where's the cereal? Hey, Dad?"

"What *what*? I'm right here."

Martin was standing with the fridge door open, staring at the empty egg rack on the inside of the door.

"No eggs," he murmured incredulously.

"Check inside. Maybe I didn't put them—hey, Dad."

"*What!?*"

"In England you know what they've got a special tax for?"

"Uh—Poles? Pole tax, get it? Funny accent, funny nameski, Brits tax you."

"Nope. 'Edible pets'. Isn't that perfect?"

"It is, actually," Martin replied softly and slammed the fridge door with his foot. He then turned, watching his balance, to open a carton of eggs, like a rare book.

"Ah," he said. "Eggs. And for starch, Ben?"

"What's 'edible'?" Ben asked.

"You," Janey told him.

The dog wagged.

"Not *you*, Doghouse Demento," Janey said. "I don't care how well you self-cook."

"So anyways," Martin said.

"So anyways," Janey said.

"A perfect day for the roof."

"Oh gawd," Janey cried. "Not the roof! Not the friggin' roof!"

"Language," Martin said. "Bagel or soft, Ben? Use your words."
"Soft."

———————

After breakfast Martin, followed by Ben, went for the ladder, which hung on the inside wall of the garage. Next yard over, the goons were gathered in the spring sun. The head goon, Gary, the one with an edge on him, had lately taken down the back fence in order to roll two pickups into the yard. Out of these he was assembling a third, from the wheels up. In a row against the rear wall of the goons' house, a two-storey white clapboard half as big again as Martin's, the goons and their girlfriends had ranged, as against a stage flat, the two seats from the trucks along with a number of steel-and-vinyl kitchen chairs. Here they sprawled—the women on laps, an arm, sometimes two arms, around a goon neck, when they weren't fetching more beer—in desultory banter with Gary, at his labour. Big speakers had been set up outside, so the heavy metal and old Creedence Clearwater was not muffled or otherwise diminished by walls.

Martin's aluminum ladder with its bright blue cord and sixteen-foot capacity fascinated Ben. When Martin clanged the end of it trying to manoeuvre it out the side door of the garage, Ben put his hands over his ears, blinking. If the goons were watching, Martin didn't look to see.

"Here we go," he said.

"Hey, Dad—" Ben was walking quickly to keep up, looking to the next yard.

"Yup?"

"Are those lady goons?"

"Keep your voice down, son."

"Are they?"

"I suppose they are."

190

Martin carried the ladder onto the back step and set it on end. Having never figured out the blue cord, he extended the ladder by hand. The claws slammed each rung as the ladder went higher. At full extension the end just made the second-storey eavestrough and this was from the elevation of the back step. Martin understood that really he ought to have a longer ladder.

He stuck his head in the back door. "Hey, Janey!"

Ben appeared, moving fast from around the side of the house. "Know what, Dad?" he said in a loud whisper.

"No, what."

"I just saw into the goons' house!"

"Good work, Ben. Any sightings?"

"What?"

"See anything?"

"No."

"Huh."

"It's old in there."

"Yeah, it's an old house, Ben. Like this one."

"What one?"

"Ours. Our house."

"Our house is nicer. Dad?"

"Yes?"

"Do the lady goons live there too?"

"Some of them."

When Janey appeared her nose was red.

"White spray on the mirror?" Martin inquired.

"Don't be gross."

Janey scowled as she stood with one foot and both hands on the ladder while Martin crawled upward. From his left wrist he had slung a yellow plastic Safeway bag containing tools and materials for patching the eavestrough and a rotted place in the facing behind it where water had been coming in, again. With both hands he held tight to the ladder. He did not like the spring of the thing. Finally his eyes were level with the edge of the shingle, but the ladder did not extend far enough beyond it to be grasped while he stepped off with dignity like a proper Mr. Fix-it. Instead he had to throw the bag up and crawl, clawing gritty shingle, over the end of the ladder—across the abysmal clinging terror of being on neither ladder nor roof—and onto the gentle, fortunately, slope.

"That's it, Janey!"

"Tell me, okay?"

Last time she'd caught him trying to ease down alone.

"So listen for the word," Martin said.

Standing on the edge of the roof, Martin could see Ben walking around the yard jabbing his shovel into the grass, stopping every once in a while to stare at the goons. Sometimes Martin felt so much love for his son that it threatened to throw him down from a high place. Dizzy, he squatted. As he did so he saw that on his garage roof a cat belonging to the old lady on the other side from the goons paced with its tail whipping. What was it doing? A blue jay watched from the grass. In the goons' back yard Gary was talking on a cellular phone as he worked. The man was constantly surrounded by friends and followers. Of course, it's the rare individual who can turn two old wrecked trucks into a perfectly good one in front of everybody's eyes. While talking on the phone.

Martin stood up. A tour of the roof. The slope was gentle by the eaves, steeper toward the central ridge. Martin stepped along close to the eaves. A little dizziness from the height. How much of vertigo is knowing you just might throw yourself over? Below, on Martin's right, the neighbour lady's roof, a quilt of windstorms and partial measures. She was very old, a new roof had not been worth it to her for a long time.

And then Martin was crouched at the window of his dormer, gazing in at a pink sea of government insulation. Last month he had been up here to measure a pane for an air vent and up again to install it. The salesclerk at the building supply, a guy with Orange

Crush hair, had kept bringing the wrong design, shape, size. As the guy was on his way to the back for the fourth time, Martin had turned to a couple of clerks smirking at the transaction and said, "The man is a fool."

The smirks vanished, the guy heard the remark. He paused, kept going. Later as he handed Martin the correct vent, he said, "I hope you choke on it."

Fair enough, Martin had thought, nodding as he took the vent from the guy's hand. Fair enough.

On the other side of the ridge, the goon side, the sewer stink of the septic tube. Higher up the slope, the shining globe ventilator, casting its flickering shadow against goon clapboard.

And so full circle. Martin came around the blanched, eroded chimney, looked at the Safeway bag, and kept going. One more time for the difference and remove. He was conscious now of the views, back and front, down through gaps in the leaves to the clipped grass, the street with its margin of dust and oil stains where the cars parked, and he got the longer ones too: the skein of trolley lines two houses over, office towers downtown in Sunday quiet, a small plane crawling the blue sky.

But mostly what Martin got was the difference, how he could never imagine it. You climb a little. Suddenly you're in the trees, new breezes. Same world, different world. Like when a cloud darkens the sun. You can't conceive how everything will be once the cloud moves away. And then it has, the sun is back, and you can't conceive how everything will be once the next cloud arrives. Sun's out, sun's in, sun's out. Inconceivable. An astronaut comes back to earth, and after all that training, all that simulation, how could anyone have known beforehand the reality of walking on the moon?

How was it, captain?

Awesome, sir.

Any ego effects at this point in time you're prepared to report on?

Yes, sir. Hunger for love, sir.

Well, captain. [Clears throat.] *I'm sure we can scare you up a little something.*

No, sir. My hunger is for the love and respect of my fellow creatures.

Full circle once more, and Martin was kneeling to dump the contents of the Safeway bag.

A car, a Trans-Am sort of thing, had pulled into the goons' back yard. Gary's girlfriend was at the wheel. It seemed that she was on her way somewhere but had failed to clear this first with Gary. It wasn't that she couldn't go, she could. It was something else. The speakers happened to be silent for a moment and Gary was five feet from the car, so Martin heard what it was.

"Your problem," Gary explained to his girlfriend, "you fuckin' snivel too much. It fuckin' grates on my nerves."

The way she sat there in the driver's seat looking up at Gary, Martin was glad he could not hear her apologizing. And then her head bowed and a metal shriek went up. She'd turned the ignition with the engine idling. That got a big cheer from everybody except Gary, who watched from deep in an aside to a buddy as she backed, goon reckless, into the lane and pulled away with a little wave of her fingers. Gary and his buddy laughed, from the stomach, at something meant to sound dirty, and Gary turned back to his work. Over goon speakers Creedence Clearwater hit the opening chords of "Proud Mary" for the nine trillionth time in the history of the world, on the garage roof the neighbour lady's cat continued to pace, and Martin thought about his dinner last night with Gwyneth, who called herself Gwen. She had worn a bottle-green cashmere suit and left with it dusted in ashes. *Clack clack clack clack* went her high heels down the walk to her car.

Gwen was older than Martin by four years, six months, and two days. He knew this because he had found her by going through the personnel files at work. Gwen was easily the most desirable unattached forty-seven-year-old woman in the company. There was only one thing, and Martin had found it out last night.

Under Gwen's house there lived ten to fifteen skunks. She had called in the City, but nothing had worked. Skunks are too smart for traps, and you can't poison them because they go back home to die and suddenly your live-skunk smell problem (the spray permeates joists and wallboard and cannot be removed) was nothing. Gwen got Martin to put his face in her purse and sure enough. They were having a drink before dinner, single malt, a fire going in the grate. She was telling him the skunk story, in episodes, like a fantastic, comic outrage against herself. Each episode seemed to be the last, and then there was another, more outrageous. The woman was like a magician, pulling more and more impossible objects from a hat. It was a wall of performance, seamless and hard. She was still at it when Martin's dog walked in, took a look around, whined, sat down, got up, sniffed, howled, and threw itself into the fireplace.

Billows of smoke and ash. With an arm over his face, Martin kept grabbing at the blur of the dog's legs while Gwen exclaimed and cried out. At last Janey ran in with a big pot of cold water and tossed it on the dog, which scrambled to its feet in a fit of uncontrollable sneezing. As soon as that subsided, it shook the water off, pelt-cracking dog style, everybody springing back, and walked out of the room, stumbling a little on the way from a kick in the ass by Martin, who turned to Gwen and said, "Look, I've been at this a long time. I don't know why it shouldn't be easy by now. I don't know why a person shouldn't be allowed to get back to something they can fucking relate to."

Gwen stayed for the meal, but she was gone right after coffee. Martin did the dishes. Then he put on his winter coat and went out into the back yard.

No stars. Too much light from the goons' back yard floodlights, the light over Martin's own back porch, the light from the dining room, the light from Janey's bedroom, the yellow light of the city sky, and the lights of the back lane. Night was aspiring to day, but it was cold. No goons out back. They had all gone to the bar. One of Gary's admirers had arrived mid-afternoon in the brand-new cab of a sixteen wheeler, now parked, minus rig, right up against the two old pickups, what was left of them, and the new one being born. The monster was silent, candy apple with silver sparkles at various depths, gleaming. It had come from another dimension. It was twice as tall as Martin's garage, half the length of the goons' back yard. It was enormously large, way, way out of scale. Martin stood and looked at it for a long time, and then he went back into the house.

———

Next day, Sunday, on his roof, squatted with his Safeway bag of trough-patching materials, Martin lifted his eyes to see how the goons' back yard looked in daytime containing the absence of a sixteen-wheeler cab. But the movement of the neighbour lady's cat on his garage roof stopped his eye, and that was when he understood what the animal was doing. Six or seven feet away was a shed roof it wanted to jump to. Would it make it? The cat didn't know. It paced and crackled. Tail switching, it returned again and again to study this problem. The knowledge it needed was more than distance, than relative heights and traction of surfaces, than force and direction of breezes. It was muscles and sinews. It was all the other jumps. Some cats do fall. It was, Exactly how much do I want this thing? It was, When will I want it enough? You focus and focus, you stoke your energy, you're practically out of your mind.

But does it really have to be this way? Look at slime mould. The kid loses interest, things dry out, there's no hesitation—up a tree, a building, up the side of the fridge. At rest in your elevated position you stretch out and wait. A breeze will come, it always does. That music you hear, the backbeat? That's not "Proud Mary", that's the sound of flowers bursting from the surface of your body.

This book is set in Garamond, a standard typeface used by book designers and printers for four centuries, and one of the finest old styles ever cut. Some characteristics of Garamond to note are the small spur on the "G", the open bowl on the "P", the curving tail on the "R", and the short lower-case height and very small counters of the "a" and "e".

The text stock is 55 lb. Windsor High-bulk Cream